MY UNCLE AND THE CURÉ

My Uncle and the Curé

By JEAN DE LA BRÈTE

Translated by
N. ST. BARBE SLADEN

NEW YORK · THE VANGUARD PRESS

MY UNCLE AND THE CURÉ

CHAPTER ONE

I AM so small that people might regard me as a dwarf, but for the fact that my head and my hands are in perfect proportion to my stature. My face is neither excessively long, nor of that ridiculous breadth attributed to dwarfs and deformed persons generally, and the delicacy of my limbs would make a pretty lady jealous.

The slenderness of my figure, however, has made me cry in secret.

I say in secret, because my lilliputian body hides a proud, haughty spirit, which is incapable of showing up its weaknesses to the first-comer . . . especially my aunt. At least, this was my way of thinking at the age of fifteen. But the events, sorrows, cares, joys, the habits of life, in short, have rapidly humbled characters more implacable than mine.

My aunt was the most disagreeable woman that I have ever known. I considered her very ugly, as far as my mind, which had seen nothing and made no comparisons, could form an opinion of the matter. Her face was angular and common, her voice loud, her step heavy, and she was ridiculously tall.

Compared with her, I looked like a greenfly or an ant. When I spoke to her, I raised my head as high as if I had wanted to examine the top of a poplar. She was of common origin and, like many of her kind, rated physical strength above everything and professed a contempt for my puny appearance which overwhelmed me.

Her mind was a faithful reproduction of her outward

appearance. It consisted of nothing but harshness, roughness and sharp angles, which the wretched people who used to live with her were up against every day.

My uncle, a country gentleman whose stupidity had become proverbial in the district, had married her out of weakness of mind and character. He died soon after his marriage and I never knew him. When I was able to think over the matter, I attributed this premature death to my aunt, who appeared to me strong enough to consign not only a poor wretch like my uncle, but also a whole regiment of husbands to their graves.

I was two years old when my parents were laid to rest, leaving me to the whims of life and to my family's trustees. My parents left a fairly good remnant of a large fortune: about four hundred thousand francs in land, which brought in a very good income.

My aunt agreed to educate me. She did not like children, but as her husband had managed things incompetently, she was badly off and thought with satisfaction of the affluence my coming to the house would bring.

What an ugly, big, dilapidated, badly-kept house; built in the middle of a courtyard, full of dung-heaps, mud, hens and rabbits. Behind it was a garden, in which all the plants in creation grew, without anybody paying it the slightest attention. I believe that within the memory of man no gardener was ever seen pruning the trees, or uprooting the weeds, which grew as they liked, without my aunt or myself troubling ourselves about them.

This primeval forest did not please me as, though a child, I had an innate idea of neatness.

The estate was called 'The Thicket'. It was situated in the depths of the country, half a league from the church and a little village consisting of about twenty cottages. There were no *châteaux* or manor-houses for five leagues round. We lived in the most complete isolation. My aunt sometimes went to C——, the town nearest 'The Thicket'. I very much wanted to go with her, so she never took me. The sole events of our life were the arrival of the farmers, who brought what they owed, or the amount of their quarterly rent, and the Curé's visits.

Oh! what a splendid man he was!

He came to the house three times a week, having undertaken, in a moment of enthusiasm, to cram my brain with every science he knew. He pursued his task perseveringly, although I knew how to try his patience. As I was not thick-headed, I learnt easily, but idleness was my besetting sin; I liked and petted it, in spite of the Curé's eloquent pains and his countless efforts to uproot this plant of Satan's from my mind.

Afterwards (and this was the most serious part of it), the faculty of arguing rapidly developed. I entered upon discussions which turned the Curé inside out; I allowed myself to make comments which often shocked and hurt his most cherished opinions.

I took a great delight in contradicting and teasing him and opposing his ideas, tastes and assertions. That stirred up my blood and kept my mind on the alert. I suspect that he felt the same, and he would have been deeply sorry if I had suddenly dropped my wrangling ways and independent ideas.

I took care, however, not to do so, for when I saw him fidgeting in his chair, ruffling his hair in despair, soiling his nose with snuff, oblivious of the rules of propriety —a forgetfulness which only occurred on serious occasions—nothing could equal my satisfaction.

3

If, however, it had only been in fun, I believe I could have sometimes resisted the tempting demon. My aunt had the disastrous habit of being present at the lessons, although she understood nothing and yawned ten times an hour.

Now contradicting, even though her ugly form was not involved, enraged her, and her anger increased all the more, as she did not dare say anything before the Curé. Furthermore, to see me arguing seemed to her comparable to a physical and moral outrage. I never attacked her directly as she was brutal and I was afraid she might hit me. Finally, my voice—although sweet and musical, I flatter myself!—produced a disastrous effect on her auditory nerves.

On these occasions, it can be imagined that it was impossible for me not to make use of my malice to infuriate my aunt and tease the Curé.

Nevertheless, I liked this poor Curé! I liked him very much and knew that in spite of my absurd arguments, which sometimes bordered on rudeness, he had the greatest affection for me. I was not only the favourite member of his flock; I was his favourite child; his work, the girl of his heart and soul. Mingled with this paternal affection was a touch of admiration for my abilities, my remarks and deeds in general.

He had taken his task to heart; he had sworn to teach me, to watch over me as a guardian angel, in spite of my mischievous brain, my logic and my whims. Moreover, this task had quickly become the sweetest event in his life, the best, if not the only distraction in his monotonous existence.

In the rain, wind, snow, hail, heat, cold and storm, I saw the Curé arrive, with his cassock tucked up to his knees and his hat under his arm. I don't know if I ever saw him with it on. He was in the habit of walking bare-headed, smiling at the passers-by, the birds, trees and blades of grass. Fat and plump, he appeared to rebound from the earth, on which he trampled with a brisk step, and to which he seemed to say: 'You are good and I like you!' He was content to be alive, satisfied with himself and satisfied with everybody. His worthy face, ruddy and fresh, surrounded by white hair, reminded me of those late roses which still bloom under the first fall of snow.

When he came into the courtyard, hens and rabbits used to run, on hearing his voice, to nibble some crusts of bread which he took care to slip into his pocket before leaving the Presbytery. Perrine, the poultry-yard maid, used to curtsy to him, and Suzon, the cook, hastened to open the door and show him into the drawing-room, where we used to have our lessons.

My aunt, installed in an armchair with all the elegance of a rather thick lightning-conductor, rose as he came in, made him welcome with a sulky air and precipitately embarked upon a list of my wrong-doings. After which, sitting down again, bolt upright, her favourite cat on her knees, she took her knitting and awaited, or rather did not await, an opportunity of saying something disagree-able to me.

The worthy Curé used to listen patiently to this rough voice, which grated on his ear. He rounded his back, as if this rebuke was intended for him, and threatened me with his finger, half smiling. Thank goodness he had known my aunt for many years.

We sat at a little table, which we had put near the window. This spot was doubly advantageous, as it kept us far enough from my aunt, who sat near the fireplace at the end of the room, and permitted my eyes to follow the flight of swallows and flies; and in winter to notice the effects of the snow and frost on the trees in the garden.

The Curé put his snuff-box beside him, a check handkerchief on the arm of his easy-chair, and the lesson began.

When my idleness was not too great, things went well, as far as exercises to be corrected were concerned, as, although as short as possible, they were always carefully done. My handwriting was neat and my style easy. The Curé used to shake his head in a satisfied manner, take snuff enthusiastically and say 'Good, very good' in all manners of intonation.

During this time I secretly counted the stains on his cassock and asked myself how he would look if he had a black wig, close-fitting knickers and a red velvet coat, like my grandfather used to wear in his portraits.

The thought of the Curé in knickers and a wig was so pleasant that I burst out laughing. My aunt exclaimed: 'Stupid little creature!' and other pleasantries of this kind, which were as civil as they were explicit.

The Curé looked at me, smiling, and repeated two or three times: 'Ah! youth, beautiful youth!'

And a retrospect of himself at the age of fifteen caused him to sigh.

After that we went on to recitation and things no longer went well. It was the momentous hour, the moment for talk, personal opinions, discussions, and indeed even disputes.

The Curé liked men of olden times, heroes, the almost incredible deeds in which physical courage played an important part. This predilection was curious, as he was not exactly moulded on the lines of a hero.

I had noticed that he did not at all like going home after dark, and this discovery made me like him all the more (as I myself was an awful coward) and did not leave me under any illusion as to his pluck.

Furthermore his worthy, calm and quiet mind, loving repose and order and loving his flock and the body which enshrined it, had absolutely never dreamt of martyrdom. I saw him grow as slightly pale as his rosy cheeks permitted as he read the list of torments inflicted on the early Christians.

He thought it very beautiful to enter Paradise with a heroic leap, but considered it very sweet to advance quietly towards eternity without fatigue or haste. He had none of those exalted outbursts, which create a desire for death, in order to see the Ruler of the world at an earlier date and time. Oh! not at all! He had made up his mind to depart without a murmur when the time came, but he sincerely wished it to be postponed as long as possible.

I confess that my character, which does not shine in an heroic light, falls in with this gentle, easy-going moral standard. He was nevertheless attached to his heroes; he admired and exalted them and liked them more especially as, doubtless, he felt that he was totally incapable of following their example.

As for me, I shared neither his tastes nor his admiration. I had a pronounced antipathy for the Greeks and Romans. Through the subtle working of my fantastic intellect I had decided that the latter were like my aunt, or that my aunt was like the latter, whichever you please, and from the day I made this comparison the Romans were tried, condemned and executed in my mind.

The Curé, however, persisted in dabbling in Roman history with me and on my part I was obstinately bent on not taking any interest in it. The men of the Republic did not impress me and my brain was confused by the Emperors. The Curé uttered his eulogistic remarks in vain, getting angry and arguing, but nothing shook my apathy and personal views.

For instance, relating the history of Mucius Scaevola, I finished thus: 'He burned his right hand to punish it for having deceived him, which proves he was only a simpleton!'

The Curé, who a moment before was looking at me sanctimoniously, trembled with anger.

'A simpleton, mademoiselle!... Why?'

'Because the loss of his hand did not atone for his mistake,' I replied. 'Porsena was not living any more or any less and the secretary did not behave any better.'

'All right, my little one; but Porsena was sufficiently frightened to raise the siege immediately.'

'That proves, Monsieur le Curé, that Porsena was nothing but a coward.'

'So be it! But Rome was delivered, thanks to whom? Thanks to Scaevola, and his heroic deed.'

And the Curé, shuddering at the thought of burning the tip of his finger, only admired Mucius Scaevola more, got excited and struggled to make me appreciate his hero.

'I adhere to what I have said,' I resumed quietly. 'He was only a simpleton, and a big one too!'

The Curé choked and exclaimed:

'When children meddle with arguments, people hear silly things.'

'Monsieur le Curé, you taught me the other day that arguing is man's greatest faculty.'

'Doubtless, doubtless, when he knows how to make use

of it. But I was speaking of grown-up men, not little girls.'

'Monsieur le Curé, a little bird tries its strength on the edge of its nest.'

The worthy man, somewhat disconcerted, ruffled his hair energetically, which gave him the appearance of a wolf's head, powdered white.

'You are wrong to argue such a lot, little one,' he used to say to me sometimes; 'it is a sin of pride. You will not always have me to answer for you and, when you are struggling with life, you will learn that you don't argue, you submit to it.'

But what did I care about life? I had a Curé on whom to practise my logic and that was sufficient for me.

When I had teased, bored and tormented him, he endeavoured to assume a severe expression, but was compelled to relinquish his project, his ever-smiling mouth totally refusing to obey him.

He then said to me:

'Mademoiselle de Lavalle, you will recapitulate the Roman Emperors, so as not to confuse Tiberius with Vespasian.'

'Let us leave these worthy men alone, Monsieur le Curé,' I replied; 'they bore me. Do you know that if you had lived in their time, they would have burnt you alive, or torn out your tongue and nails, or cut you in little slender pieces, like a meat pasty!'

The Curé trembled slightly at this gloomy picture and trotted away without deigning to reply.

I knew that his dissatisfaction had reached its height when he called me Mademoiselle de Lavalle. This formal name was the clearest way of showing it and I regretted it until I saw him appear once more, his hair blown about by the wind and a smile on his lips.

9

CHAPTER TWO

MY aunt used to terrorize me when I was a child and I feared blows to such a degree that I obeyed without arguing.

On my sixteenth birthday she hit me for the last time. From that day onwards, so epoch-making in my intimate life, a rebellion which had been stirring secretly in my mind for some months suddenly broke out and completely changed my attitude towards my aunt.

At that time the Curé and I re-read the history of France and I flatter myself that I knew it very well. Considering the omissions and limitations of my textbook, my knowledge was certainly as extensive as possible.

The Curé had a love for his Kings almost amounting to veneration. He did not, however, like Francis I. This dislike was all the more remarkable as Francis I was brave and remained popular. But he did not suit the Curé, who never lost an opportunity of criticizing him and, out of love of contradicting, I chose him as my favourite.

On the day I mentioned above, I had to recite the lesson about my friend. The day before, I sought for a long time a means of making him rise in the Curé's estimation. Unfortunately, I could only repeat the phrases in my history book, uttering opinions which savoured more of an impression than an argument.

I had racked my brains in thought for an hour, when a brilliant idea crossed my mind. 'The library!' I exclaimed. Immediately I ran down a long passage and for the first time entered a medium-sized room, entirely lined with book-shelves joined together by the thin threads of a large number of cobwebs. It communicated with the rooms which had been closed after my uncle's death, never to be entered again; it smelt so musty that I was nearly suffocated. I hastened to open the window, which, being very small, had neither bolts nor Venetian shutters, and overlooked the wildest corner of the garden. I then started my investigations. But how was I to find Francis I amongst all those books?

I was about to give up my plan when the title of a small book made me cry out with joy. It contained the biographies of the Kings of France up to Henry IV. A fairly good engraving, depicting Francis I in the magnificent dress of the Valois, was also included in the biography. I examined it in astonishment.

'Is it possible,' I exclaimed, amazed, 'that there are men as handsome as that?'

The biography, which did not share the Curé's antipathy for my hero, praised him unreservedly. It spoke with enthusiastic conviction of his handsome face, his bravery, his chivalrous manners and the enlightened protection which he bestowed on literature and the arts. It concluded with two lines, referring to his private life, and I learned something of which I was totally ignorant—namely, that:

'Francis I led a happy life and liked women tremendously. He had a great and sincere partiality for a beautiful lady, Anne de Pisseleu, to whom he gave the County of Étampes, which he raised to a Duchy, to give her special gratification.'

From these words I drew the following conclusions: firstly, having discovered for the last month that my life was monotonous, that I lacked a good many things, that possessing a Curé, an aunt, fowls and rabbits were not sufficient happiness, I decided that a happy life was evidently the antithesis of mine and Francis I displayed sound judgment in choosing it; secondly, that he certainly possessed the holy virtue of charity, preached by my Curé, since he liked women so much; thirdly, that Anne de Pisseleu was a happy individual and that I should have liked a King to give me a County, raised to a Duchy to 'give me special gratification'.

'Bravo!' I exclaimed, throwing the book up to the ceiling and catching it again adroitly. 'Here is the means of confounding the Curé and converting him to my way of thinking.'

In the evening, in bed, I re-read the little biography.

'What a fine man Francis I was!' I thought. 'But why does the author speak only of his love of women? Why did he not also write of his love of men? After all, each one to his taste! But if I judge women by my aunt, I think I should have a decided predilection for men.'

Then I recalled the fact that the biography was written by one of the male sex and thought that he had doubtless considered it polite, agreeable and modest to pass over himself and his fellow-men in silence. I fell asleep with this enlightening idea.

The next day I got up, feeling very pleased. Firstly, I was sixteen years old; secondly, the little creature who looked at herself in the glass saw a face not displeasing to her. I then made two or three pirouettes, thinking of the Curé's consternation at my new knowledge.

In my impatience I had sat at my table for a fairly long time when he arrived, pink and smiling. At the sight of him, my heart thumped somewhat like that of a great captain on the eve of a battle.

'Now then, little one,' he said, when my exercises were corrected and he had made a grimace at their conciseness, 'let us pass on to Francis I and examine him in all his aspects.'

He settled down comfortably in his armchair, took his snuff-box in one hand, his handkerchief in the other, and looking askance at me, made preparations for keeping up the discussion which he foresaw was imminent. I started on my subject from the beginning. I got restless, lively and enthusiastic. I dwelt at length on the qualities set forth in my history book, after which I passed on to my intimate knowledge.

'What a charming man, Monsieur le Curé! His figure was full of majesty, his face noble and handsome, such a pretty beard, trimmed to a point, and such beautiful eyes!'

I paused for a moment for breath, and the startled Curé, drawing himself up stiffly, like a little imp on springs in a cardboard box, exclaimed:

'Where have you learned this nonsense, mademoiselle?'

'That's my secret,' I said with a mysterious little smile. And burning my boats, I continued:

'Monsieur le Curé, I don't know what poor Francis I has done to you! Are you aware that he was a fine judge of things? He led a merry life and was passionately fond of women.'

The Curé's eyes then opened so wide that I was afraid they would burst. He exclaimed: 'Saint Michael! Saint Barnabas!' and dropped his snuff-box with such a sudden noise that the cat, which was stretched out in its basket, jumped on to the floor with a despairing miaow.

My aunt, who was asleep, started up and exclaimed, 'Ugly creature!'—addressing her remark to me, not to the cat, without knowing what it was about. But this epithet invariably formed the beginning and the peroration of all her speeches. I certainly expected great results to follow. I remained somewhat nonplussed, however, in view of the Curé's expression, which was really extraordinary. But I soon began again, unperturbed: 'He was particularly fond of a beautiful lady, to whom he gave a duchy. Confess, Monsieur le Curé, that he was an excellent man and that it would have been very pleasant to have been in Anne de Pisseleu's place.'

'Holy Virgin!' exclaimed the Curé in a subdued voice. 'The child is mad!'

'What's the matter?' said my aunt, piercing her chignon with one of her knitting needles. 'Send her out of the room if she is impertinent.'

'My child,' continued the Curé, 'where did you learn what you have just said?'

'In a book,' I replied briefly, without mentioning the library.

'How can you repeat such abominable things?'

'Abominable things?' I exclaimed, horrified. 'Well, Monsieur le Curé, you think it is abominable that Francis I was generous and was fond of women? You don't like them then?'

'What is she saying?' roared my aunt, who, after listening to me attentively for a few minutes, prophesied the most disastrous results from my question. 'Impertinent youngster, you . . .'

'Peace, my dear lady, peace!' interrupted the Curé, appearing to be relieved of a great weight. 'Let me explain to Reine. Come now, what do you consider praiseworthy in the conduct of Francis I?'

'Really, it is quite simple!' I answered, somewhat scornfully, reflecting that the Curé was ageing and was beginning to be slow of comprehension. 'You preach daily love of one's neighbour, and it seems to me that Francis I put your favourite theory into practice. Love your neighbour as yourself, for the love of God.'

I had hardly concluded my remark before the Curé, after wiping his face, on which were great beads of perspiration, turned over in his armchair and, with both hands on his stomach, indulged in a Homeric laugh of such long duration that tears of vexation and annoyance came into my eyes.

'I have been very foolish indeed,' I said in a quivering voice, 'to give myself so much trouble to learn my lesson and make you like Francis I.'

'My dear young child,' he said to me at length, resuming a serious manner and assuming the favourite look he reserved for occasions when he was pleased with me. 'What amazes me so much, my dear little child, is that I did not know you so much admired people who practise the virtue of charity.'

'In any case, there's nothing to laugh at,' I replied sulkily.

'Come, come. Don't let us get angry.'

And the Curé, giving me a tap on the cheek, cut the lesson short, told me he would return the next day and forthwith proceeded to confiscate the key of the library, about which (he left me in no doubt) he knew everything. He had not yet left the courtyard when my aunt flew at me and shook me hard enough to dislocate my shoulder.

'Ugly hussy! what have you said and done to make the Curé leave so early?'

'Why are you angry,' I said, 'if you don't know what it is about?'

'Oh, I don't know! Considering I heard what you said to the Curé, rude child?'

Judging that mere words ill-sufficed to give vent to her wrath, she slapped me, hit me hard and put me outside, like a dog. I fled to my room and barricaded myself effectively. My first care was to take off my dress and to prove in the glass that my aunt's dry, thin fingers had left blue marks on my shoulders. 'Wretched little slave,' I said, shaking my fist at my reflection in the glass, 'will you put up with such things any longer? Is cowardice to prevent your daring to rebel!' I admonished myself severely for some minutes, and then the reaction set in and I fell into a chair and wept copiously.

'What have I done,' I thought, 'to be treated like this? The ugly woman!' Then, again, why had the Curé made such a funny face during my lesson? And I began to laugh whilst tears were still flowing down my cheeks. But in vain did I probe the problem. I found no solution to it. Going to the open window, I looked sadly at the garden, and I was beginning to regain my calm when I seemed to recognize the voice of my aunt, talking to Suzon. I leant out a little to listen to their conversation.

'You are wrong,' said Suzon. 'The little girl is no longer a child. If you are rough towards her, she will complain to M. de Pavol, who will take her to live with him.'

'I should like to see that happen! But how do you imagine that she will think of her uncle? She barely knows of his existence.'

'Bah! The girl is sly! She only needs to refresh her

memory for a moment to send you about your business if you make her unhappy, and her fine income will disappear with her.'

'Well, we shall see. . . . I won't beat her again, but. . . .'

They moved away and I did not hear the conclusion of the sentence. After dinner, at which I refused to appear, I went to find Suzon. She had been my aunt's friend before becoming her cook. They had disputes ten times a day, but could not do without one another. I should hardly be believed if I said that Suzon sincerely liked her mistress; it is, however, perfectly true. But if she forgave my aunt's social elevation, she doubtless blamed the next best thing, her circumstances and her life, for she was always grumbling. She had the surly expression of a footpad, and always wore short under-petticoats and flat-heeled shoes, although she never went to town to sell milk and her imagination did not run away with her like Perrine's .

'Suzon,' I said to her, deliberately standing in front of her, 'am I rich then?'

'Who told you that nonsense, mademoiselle?'

'That is no business of yours, Suzon; but I want you to answer me: Where does Uncle de Pavol live?'

'All right, all right,' grumbled Suzon. 'She's no longer a child, 'pon my word! Run away, mademoiselle! I won't tell you anything, because I know nothing.'

'You lie, Suzon, and I forbid you to answer me like that. I heard what you were saying to my aunt just now !'

'Well, if you heard, mademoiselle, it is not worth while making me speak.'

Suzon turned her back on me and would not answer any of my questions. I went up to my room again, very annoyed, and remained for a long time with my elbows on the window-sill. I called the moon, stars and trees to witness that I irrevocably resolved not to allow myself to be whipped and not to be afraid of my aunt, and to adopt every means of being disagreeable to her. And, dropping the petals of a flower, from which I was pulling the leaves, I flung my fears, my pusillanimity and former bashfulness to the winds. I felt that I was no longer the same person and fell asleep, comforted. In the night I dreamt that my aunt, changed into a dragon, was fighting Francis I, who killed her with his huge sword. He took me in his arms and flew away with me, whilst the Curé looked at us despondently and wiped his face with his check handkerchief. He afterwards twisted it with all his might and the perspiration trickled from it, as if it had been dipped in the river.

CHAPTER THREE

THE next day the Curé and I had hardly taken our places at table when the door opened with a crash and we saw Perrine come in, her bonnet on the back of her neck and her clogs, stuffed with straw, in her hand.

'Is the house on fire?' said my aunt.

'No, ma'am. But the Devil is here for a certainty! The cow is in the barley field, which was growing so well; she is ruining everything. I can't catch her; the capons are on the roof and the rabbits in the kitchen-garden.'

'In the kitchen-garden!' cried my aunt, rising and casting an angry glance at me, for the said kitchen-garden was for her a sacred spot and the centre of her only affections.

'My beautiful capons,' grumbled Suzon, who thought it opportune to appear and add her snappy tones to the cries of her mistress.

'You silly woman!' said my aunt.

She quickly followed in the wake of her servants, angrily slamming the door.

'Monsieur le Curé,' I said immediately, 'do you think it possible for there to be any woman in this world as vile as my aunt?'

'Well, well, little one, what does that mean?'

'Do you know what she did yesterday, Monsieur le Curé? She beat me!'

'Beat you!' exclaimed the Curé incredulously, so impossible did it appear to him that anyone should dare to touch a little creature as delicate as me with so much as a little finger.

'Yes, beat me; and if you don't believe me, I am going to show you the traces of her blows.'

At these words I began to unbutton my dress. The Curé looked straight in front of him in a scared way.

'It is useless, useless! I take your word for it,' he exclaimed hurriedly, red in the face and chastely lowering his eyes to the tips of his shoes.

'Beating me on my sixteenth birthday!' I resumed as I did up my dress. 'Do you know that I loathe her?' And I struck the table with my clenched fist, which hurt me very much.

'Come, come, my little child,' said the Curé, quite touched. 'Be calm and relate what you had done.'

'Nothing at all. When you had gone, she called me a shameless girl and flung herself on me, like a fury. The ugly woman.'

'Come, Reine, come. You know you must forgive your injuries.'

'What next?' I exclaimed, roughly drawing back my chair and taking large strides up and down the drawing-room. 'I shall never forgive her!'

The Curé rose in turn and began to walk in the opposite direction to me, so that we continued our conversation as we kept crossing one another's path, just like the giant and Tom Thumb when the latter stole one of the seven-league boots and the monster was pursuing him.

'You must be reasonable, Reine, and submit to this humiliation penitently for the remission of your sins.'

'My sins?' I said, stopping, and slightly shrugging my shoulders. 'You know, Monsieur le Curé, that they are so small that they are not worth talking about.'

'Indeed,' said the Curé, unable to repress a smile. 'Since you are a saint, submit to your trials in patience for the love of God.'

'No, indeed!' I replied in a determined manner. 'I wish to love God a little . . . not too much. Don't frown, Monsieur le Curé, but I understand that He loves me sufficiently to be dissatisfied when He sees me unhappy.'

'What a brain,' exclaimed the Curé. 'What an education I have given you!'

'In short,' I continued as I started walking up and down again, 'I want to have my revenge, and have it I shall!'

'That is very wicked, Reine. Be quiet and listen to me.'

'Vengeance is the sport of the gods,' I replied, jumping to catch a large fly which was buzzing round my head.

'Let us talk seriously, little one.'

'But I am talking seriously,' I said, pausing for a minute in front of a glass, to prove, with a certain amount of self-satisfaction, that excitement suited me very well. 'You will see, Monsieur le Curé! I shall take a sword and behead my aunt, as Judith did to Holophernes.'

'This child has gone mad!' exclaimed the Curé sadly. 'Remain quiet for a little while, mademoiselle, and don't talk nonsense.'

'All right, Monsieur le Curé, but confess that Judith wasn't worth a penny?'

The Curé leant against the mantelpiece and delicately applied a pinch of snuff to his nostrils.

'Excuse me, little one; that depends on the circumstances in which you are placed.'

'How illogical you are!' I said. 'You consider Judith's action magnificent, because she delivered a few wicked

Israelites, who were certainly nothing to me and ought to be of scant interest to you, seeing that they are dead and have been buried so long! And you would strongly disapprove of my doing as much for my own deliverance! Goodness knows, I am very much alive!' I added, spinning round on my heels several times.

'You have a good opinion of yourself,' replied the Curé, who endeavoured to assume a grave attitude.

'Ah! that's good.'

'Come. Do you wish to listen to me now?'

'I am certain,' I said, continuing my idea, 'that Holophernes was infinitely nicer than my aunt, and that I should have got on with him perfectly. Consequently, I do not exactly see what prevents my imitating Judith.'

'Reine!' exclaimed the Curé, stamping his foot.

'My dear Curé, I beg you, don't get angry. Rest assured I shall not kill my aunt. I have another mode of vengeance.'

'Tell me about it,' said the worthy man, already appeased, flinging himself on to a sofa. I sat down beside him.

'There! You have heard of my Uncle de Pavol?'

'Certainly; he lives near V——.'

'Very well. What is the name of his estate?'

'Le Pavol.'

'Well then, if I wrote to my uncle at the Château Le Pavol, near V——, the letter would arrive safely, wouldn't it?'

'Undoubtedly.'

'Well, Monsieur le Curé, I have found my revenge. You know, even if my aunt dislikes me, she is fond of my money.'

'But how have you found that out, child?' said the Curé confusedly.

'I heard her talking to herself, so I am sure of what I say. What she fears first and foremost is that I shall complain to Monsieur de Pavol and ask to be taken into his house. I am thinking of threatening her with a letter to my uncle; and I won't say,' I added after a moment's reflection, 'that one day or other I shan't do so.'

'Well, it sounds harmless enough,' said the Curé, smiling.

'You see, you approve,' I exclaimed, clapping. 'You approve!'

'Up to a certain point, *ma petite*, yes, as it is obvious that you ought not to be struck; but I forbid impertinence. Do not use your weapon except in case of lawful defence, and remember that if your aunt has her faults, you ought to respect her and not be aggressive.'

I made an expressive face.

'I promise nothing . . . or, rather, to be candid, I promise to do the exact opposite of what you have just said.'

'This is absolute rebellion! . . . I shall end by being angry, Reine.'

'It is more than a rebellion,' I replied gravely; 'it is a revolution.'

'I shall lose patience and my life,' muttered the Curé. 'Mademoiselle de Lavalle, please me by submitting to my authority.'

'Listen,' I retorted in a wheedling tone. 'I like you with all my heart; you are the only person I like in the world.'

The Curé's face brightened up.

'But I loathe and execrate my aunt; my feelings in the

matter will never alter. I have a good deal more character than she has. . . .'

At this juncture the Curé, whose expression had become gloomy, interrupted me with a lively exclamation.

'Don't protest,' I continued, looking down at him. 'You know you are of my opinion.'

'What an education! What an education!' muttered the Curé piteously.

'Monsieur le Curé, my salvation is uncompromised, rest assured; some day or other I shall find you again in Heaven. I repeat: having much more character than my aunt, it will be easy for me to torment her verbally. Last night I promised myself to be very disagreeable to her. I called the moon and stars to witness my oath.'

'My child,' said the Curé seriously, 'you don't wish to listen to me and you will be sorry for it.'

'Bah! we shall see about that! . . . I understand my aunt; she is furious, as it is I who let out the cow, the rabbits and the capons, so as to be alone with you. Give her a lecture, Monsieur le Curé. I assure you she has beaten me terribly; I have black marks on my shoulders.'

My aunt came in like a hurricane, and the Curé, completely stupefied, had no time to answer me.

'Reine, come here,' she cried, her face purple with rage and the disorderly chase she had had after the rabbits.

I made a profound bow.

'I leave you with the Curé,' I said, making a knowing sign to my ally. The window was open, as luck would have it.

I jumped on to a chair, got on to the sill and slid into the garden, to the intense astonishment of my aunt, who was standing in front of the door to cut off my escape. I admit that I pretended to run away, but in reality I hid behind a laurel and experienced a paroxysm of unparalleled joy, listening to the Curé's reproaches and my aunt's angry remarks.

In the evening during dinner she assumed the gracious air of a mastiff which has just been given a bone. She grumbled at Suzon and sent her about her business, ill-treated her cat, and threw the silver plate on to the table, making a frightful noise; finally, exasperated by my calm, mocking manner, she seized a water-bottle and flung it out of the window. I immediately seized a dish of rice, which she had not yet tasted, and flung it in the wake of the water-bottle.

'Miserable blockhead!' cried my aunt, flinging herself on me.

'Don't come near me,' I said, stepping back. 'If you touch me, I shall write this very evening to my Uncle de Pavol.'

'Ah!' said my aunt, standing petrified with her arm raised.

'If it isn't this evening,' I continued, 'it will be to-morrow, or in a few days, as I do not wish to be beaten.'

'Your uncle won't believe you!' cried my aunt.

'Oh yes, he will! . . . Your fingers have left their marks on my shoulders. I know that he is a good soul, and I shall go away with him.'

I certainly had no idea of my uncle's character, having been only six years old when I saw him for the first and last time. But I thought that I ought to make it appear that I knew all about him and was displaying great diplomacy. I left the room majestically, leaving my aunt to pour out her heart to Suzon.

CHAPTER FOUR

WAR was declared, and from that time onward I spent my time fighting Madame de Lavalle. In former days I hardly dared to speak in her presence, except when the Curé made a third party: she imposed silence on me, even before I had finished my remark.

I should like to point out that this mode of procedure was particularly painful to me, as I am such a chatterbox. I made up for it a little with the Curé, but it was totally insufficient. I had also formed a habit of soliloquizing. I often found myself standing in front of the looking-glass, talking to my reflection for hours on end. . . . My dear glass! Faithful friend! Confidant of my secret thoughts! I do not know if men have ever seriously realized the enormous influence this little article of furniture can wield on the mind. Please note that I do not settle the sex of the owner's mind, as I am convinced that individuals with beards keep up the pleasure of looking at their outward appearance just as much as we do.

Were I to write a philosophical work, I should discourse upon this problem: 'Of the influence of the looking-glass on the intelligence and heart of man.' I do not deny that my dissertation would perhaps be unique of its kind, that it would in no way resemble the philosophy in which Kant, Fichte, Schilling, etc., floundered all their lives to their greater glory and the intense happiness of posterity, which reads them with all the more pleasure because it does not understand anything about the subject. No, my dissertation would not follow in the footsteps of these gentlemen: it would be explicit, clear, practical and of pungent piquancy; and love of contradiction would have to be pushed pretty far not to admit that these qualities are not the appanage of the above-mentioned philosophy. But as I do not consider my intelligence mature enough for this great piece of work, I am content to preserve a sincere affection for my looking-glass and to look at myself in it for a very long time each day, to show my gratitude. I am fully aware that, in view of this disclosure, some of those angry, surly individuals, who take a gloomy view of everything, will insinuate that coquetry plays a leading part in the feeling I claim to have for my looking-glass. Goodness me, people aren't perfect! And notice, dear reader, that if you are genuine, which is not certain, you will confess that personal interest (not to use a longer phrase) takes first place in most of your thoughts. To return to the subject, I would say that, having completely done with my old terrors, I did not attempt to curb my loquacity before my aunt. Not a meal went by without our having disputes, which threatened to degenerate into storms.

Although I did not yet know her origin, I soon dis-covered that she was as ignorant as a carp and that she experienced extreme vexation when I backed my opinions from my own knowledge or that of the Curé. I also never hesitated to give the title of an historical account to ideas from my own brain. Unfortunately, it was impossible for me to struggle against my aunt's personal experience and, when she declared that things occurred in such and such a fashion in the world, that men were not much more than blackguards, imps of Satan, I was furious, as I could not reply. I had sufficient sense to

27

grasp that the individuals with whom I was living could only give me a very imperfect idea of the human race in the ordinary circumstances of life.

The Curé dined with us every Sunday. He doubtless had secret reasons for not extolling the King of Creation before me, save when it was a question of his ancient heroes, whose enterprising spirit he no longer feared, for he only made extremely weak denials to my aunt's statements. The dinner on Sunday invariably consisted of a capon or fowl, a salad made of hard-boiled eggs and clotted cream, when in season. The Curé, who ate very frugally in his own house and whose palate could appreciate Suzon's cooking, used to arrive rubbing his hands and crying out with hunger.

We sat down quickly to table and the opening conversation was no less invariable than the menu.

'It is a fine day,' my aunt would say, which phrase, if it were raining, was only changed by another epithet.

'Grand weather!' the Curé used to reply cheerfully. 'It is nice to walk in this lovely sun.'

If it had rained or snowed, if there had been a frost, if it had hailed stones or sulphur, the Curé would have expressed similar satisfaction, either dwelling upon the comfort of a warm, snug room or singing the praises of a bright fire.

'But it isn't warm,' my aunt retorted. 'It is astonishing; in my time people wore white dresses at Easter.'

'Did white dresses suit you admirably?' I asked eagerly.

My aunt, who foresaw some impertinence, crushed me with a repressive look before replying: 'Certainly. Very well indeed.'

'Oh!' I exclaimed in a tone which left no doubt as to my inward convictions.

'In my time,' my aunt declared, 'young girls only spoke when they were questioned.'

'Didn't you speak in your youth, Aunt?'

'When I was questioned, not otherwise.'

'Were all young girls like you, Aunt?'

'Certainly.'

'What a wretched age we live in,' I sighed, raising my eyes heavenwards.

The Curé looked at me reproachfully and Madame de Lavalle let her glance wander over articles which covered the table, evidently tempted to fling some of them at my head.

At this juncture the conversation, which had become acute, suddenly dropped until the moment when my aunt's bitter feelings, suppressed by the efforts of her will, suddenly burst out like a machine subjected to too strong a pressure. She vented her wrath on the world at large. Men, women, and children—all went through it. At the conclusion of dinner, nothing remained of these poor human beings but a horrible mixture, not of bone and bruised flesh, but monsters of every kind.

'Men are not worth a straw,' said my aunt in her characteristically harmonious, elegant phraseology.

The Curé, who had the distressing certainty of not being a woman, kept his head bent and appeared full of contrition.

'What wretches! What scoundrels!' she resumed, looking at me furiously, as if I had belonged to the species in question.

'Hum!' answered the Curé.

'People who only think of enjoyment and eating,' continued my aunt, who had in mind the poverty bequeathed by her husband. 'What devil's imps!'

'Hum! hum!' resumed the Curé, shaking his head.

'Monsieur le Curé,' I exclaimed impatiently. 'Hum! is not a very strong argument.'

'Excuse me, excuse me,' replied the worthy man, disturbed in tasting his dinner; 'I think Madame de Lavalle exceeds the limits of her thought, when using that expression—imps of Satan. But it is quite certain that many men do not inspire much confidence.'

'You are like Francis I, you prefer women,' I said in my candid way.

'*Palsambleu!*' exclaimed my aunt, who had replaced certain very lively expressions by this phrase, borrowed from her husband, and which appeared to her to be quite aristocratic. 'Be quiet, foolish girl!'

But the Curé made a mysterious sign to her and the worthy lady bit her lips.

'And your heroes, Monsieur le Curé? And your Greeks and Romans?'

'Oh! the men of the present day do not much resemble those of former times,' said the Curé, quite convinced that he uttered a profound truth.

'And the Curés?' I continued.

'Curés are not concerned in the matter,' he replied, smiling.

This form of conversation, full of innuendoes, had the knack of irritating me extremely. I was conscious that a world of ideas and sentiments, which I ought not to delay discovering, was closed to me. I had doubts as to the absolute justice of my aunt's judgment on humanity, but I conceived that I was ignorant of many things and that I ran the risk of wallowing in my ignorance for some time.

One morning, when I was reflecting on this lamentable situation, the idea occurred to me to consult the three individuals whom I was able to see every day: John the farmer, Perrine and Suzon.

As the latter had lived at C——, I decided that her views ought to be based on wide experience and I kept her as a *bonne bouche*.

Wrapping myself in a hood, I took my clogs and wended my way to the farm, which was a kilometre from the house. Paddling along, splashing and sinking in, I arrived where John was; the farmer was cleaning his plough.

'Good day, John.'

'Good day, mamselle,' said John, doffing his woollen cap, which enabled his hair to stand up on end. When his hair was not subjected to some pressure or other, it was a peculiarity of its temperament to indulge in this little pastime.

'I have come to consult you about a very, very important matter,' I said, laying stress on the adverb to arouse his intelligence, which I knew was liable to run riot when he was interrogated.

'At your service, mamselle.'

'My aunt declares that all men are scoundrels; what is your opinion on this subject, John?'

'Scoundrels?' repeated John, his eyes open wide, as if he perceived a monster before him.

'Yes; but it is my aunt's opinion and I want yours.'

'Well, it isn't at all unlikely, all the same!'

'But that isn't an opinion, John! Come, do you think that men are usually scoundrels—yes or no?'

John put the first finger of his right hand on the end of his nose, which, as is well known, is a sign of deep meditation. After quite a minute's reflection, he made this clear and decisive answer:

'Listen, mamselle, and I'll tell you. It might well be so, but, on the other hand, it might not be so!'

'Blockhead!' I said to him, enraged at contemplating such a phenomenon of stupidity. He opened his eyes, mouth and hands—in fact he would have opened his entire person if he could have done so, in order the better to manifest his astonishment.

I returned to the courtyard of 'The Thicket', raving against the mud, my clogs, John and myself.

'Perrine,' I exclaimed, 'come here.'

Perrine, who was cleaning her dairy dishes, immediately ran up with a handful of nettles in her hand; her arms were bare, her face was as red as a small red apple and her hat was on the back of her head as usual.

'What is your opinion of men?' I said brusquely.

'Of men?'

And Perrine, having changed from an apple to a peony, let her nettles drop, took the corner of her apron, raised her left leg and remained perched on the right, looking at me, astonished.

'Come, answer! What do you think of men?'

'Mamselle wants to laugh, for sure!'

'No; I am speaking seriously. Answer quickly.'

'Well, mamselle,' said Perrine, putting herself straight on both legs, 'when they are fine fellows, I consider there are things more disagreeable to look at.'

This mode of viewing the question made me reflect deeply.

'I am not speaking of men's outward appearance,' I continued, shrugging my shoulders, 'but of their mental faculties.'

'I find them very agreeable forsooth,' answered Perrine, her little eyes gleaming.

'What! You don't consider them miscreants, scoundrels, Satan's imps?'

Perrine grinned from ear to ear. 'You see, mamselle, talking of miscreants is so sweet that . . .'

At this juncture she interrupted herself to give her head a good punch. She twisted her apron, lowered her eyes and appeared to me disposed to scamper away.

'What then? Finish what you were saying!'

'Mamselle is going to make me talk rubbish for certain; so I am off.' And, making me a most magnificent bow, she disappeared into the depths of her dairy, the door of which she shut in my face.

'Why should she talk nonsense? . . . Come! Suzon is my last resource; it remains to be seen if she will talk.'

I entered the kitchen. Suzon, armed with a broom, was getting ready to put it into active use. It seemed to me this was one of her gloomy days and I considered it would be diplomatic to adopt a few oratorical precautions before putting my question to her.

'How fine your copper things are and how they shine!' I said graciously.

'I do what I can,' grumbled Suzon. 'After all, those who are discontented have only to say so.'

'You succeed famously with fricassée of chicken, Suzon,' I continued without being discouraged; 'you ought to teach me how to prepare it.'

'It isn't your job, mademoiselle; remain at home and leave me in peace in my kitchen.' As my corrupt methods produced no result, I turned my batteries on to another point.

'Do you know this, Suzon? You must have been very pretty when you were young,' I said, reflecting that if I had been her husband, I should have put her to cook in the oven to be rid of her. I had touched a sensitive chord, for Suzon deigned to smile.

'Everyone has her day, mademoiselle.'

'Suzon,' I continued, profiting by this sudden mollification to get more rapidly to the point, 'I want to ask you a question! What is your opinion of men . . . and women?' I added, thinking it ingenious to extend my studies to both sexes. Suzon leant on her broom, assumed her sternest demeanour and answered with captivating conviction: 'Women, mademoiselle, aren't much, but men are nothing at all.'

'Oh!' I protested. 'Are you sure of that?'

'As certain as I tell you so, mademoiselle!'

She swept away the vegetable débris on the ground with as much skill as if it represented hated two-legged creatures. I retired to my room to meditate on the misanthropic axiom enunciated by Suzon, sufficiently discouraged that I wasn't of much account and that my unknown friends, men, deserved the humiliating name of 'nothing at all'.

CHAPTER FIVE

NEVERTHELESS, as my studies of customs seemed quite insufficient to me, I resolved to pursue them with the aid of the novels in the library.

One Monday—market day, to be exact—my aunt, the Curé and Suzon were due to go together to C——. My aunt had decided, as usual, that I should remain in Perrine's charge, and for the first time in my life this decision delighted me. I was sure of being left to myself, Perrine being far more occupied with her cow than with my inspirations.

For this kind of excursion the farmer used to bring round a sort of jaunting-car (known in the country as a *maringote*) to the courtyard at eight o'clock in the morning. My aunt used to appear dressed in her best clothes, wearing a round hat of black felt, to which she had added some delicate violet-coloured strings. She wore it in style on the top of her *chignon*. She was wrapped in furs, whether the weather was warm or cold, having since her marriage adopted the principle that a lady of good social position should not go out without wearing the skin of some animal or other. Thus clothed, she firmly believed that all the defects which betrayed her origins were effaced. She used to sit on a chair at the bottom of the *maringote*, the said chair being covered by a pillow, so that that delicate portion of the human frame, which an honest pen refuses to mention, might not be injured. Suzon, detailed to drive a horse which drove itself unaided, sat on the right on the front seat and the

Curé got up next to her. Then simultaneously they turned towards me.

'Don't do anything foolish,' said my aunt, 'and don't go into the kitchen-garden.'

'Don't untidy my kitchen,' cried Suzon, 'and be content with cold veal for lunch.'

The Curé said nothing, but gave me a friendly smile and made a sign, which was meant to convey to me: 'She wouldn't hear of it, but I would have taken you too.'

On this memorable Monday things happened as usual. I went a little way along the road and saw them disappear, all three jolted as if in Black Marias.

Without losing a minute, I carried out a plan which had been maturing for some time. It was a question of taking possession of the library, the key of which the Curé had unfortunately taken into his head to take away, but I was not a girl to be put out by such a trifle. I ran to look for a ladder, which I dragged under the library window; after superhuman efforts, I succeeded in raising it and resting it firmly against the wall. Climbing nimbly up the rungs, I broke a window-pane with a stone with which I had provided myself; then, removing the pieces of glass which still adhered to the window frame, I passed my head and shoulders through the aperture and slid into the library. I fell head-first on to the floor (I received an enormous bruise on my forehead and the next day the Curé brought me some ointment to heal it). My first care, after I had got up and the dizziness caused by my fall had disappeared, was to rummage in the drawers of an old bureau to discover a key similar to the one which the Curé had spirited away. My search was not a long one and, after one or two fruitless attempts,

I found what I wanted. Having as far as possible covered up the traces of my house-breaking, I settled down in an armchair, and, whilst I was resting from my labours, my attention was attracted by the works of Walter Scott on the shelf facing me. I selected one of them at random and departed to my room, bearing with me, like a treasure, a copy of *The Fair Maid of Perth*.

I had never read a novel in my life and I fell into a state of ecstasy and delight beyond my powers of description. Were I to follow the example of Methuselah and live nine hundred and sixty-nine years, I should never forget my impressions after reading *The Fair Maid of Perth*.

I experienced all the joy of a prisoner transported from his cell into the midst of trees, flowers and the sun; or, better still, the joy of a composer who hears the work of his heart and intellect played for the first time and in an ideal manner. The world, which was unknown to me, and for which I sighed unconsciously, was suddenly revealed. A light was created within me so suddenly that I thought in the past I must have been stupid and idiotic. I was intoxicated with this novel, which was so full of colour, life and energy.

In the evening I came downstairs, dreaming, to the dining-room, where the Curé, who was dining with us, awaited me impatiently. He looked at my face with profound sympathy and with the greatest interest asked me how the accident had happened.

'An accident?' I said, as if astonished.

'Your forehead is all black, my little Reine.'

'The foolish creature must have climbed a tree or up a ladder,' said my aunt.

'Yes, that's right; a ladder,' I replied.

'My poor child!' exclaimed the Curé sadly, 'you fell on your head?' I made a sign in the affirmative.

'Have you put on some arnica, little one?'

'Bah! Is it worth while?' resumed my aunt. 'Have your soup, Monsieur le Curé, and do not concern yourself with this giddy girl; she has got what she deserves.'

The Curé remained silent: he made a little friendly sign and looked at me stealthily. I did not, however, pay much attention to what was happening around me. I was thinking of that charming Catherine Glover, of that gallant Henry Smith, who fascinated me, and lo! and behold, without the slightest preamble, I burst into tears.

'Goodness me!' exclaimed the Curé, rising with alacrity. 'My dear Reine, my little child.'

'Let her be!' said my aunt. 'She is dissatisfied because she did not accompany us to C——.'

The Curé, however, who was aware that I detested crying and that I was too proud to display before my aunt annoyance of which she was the cause, approached me and asked in a low voice why I was crying and endeavoured to comfort me.

'It is nothing, my dear Curé,' I said, drying my tears and beginning to laugh. 'I abhor physical suffering. You see, I have a headache and I must look a sight.'

'Not more than usual,' said my aunt.

The Curé looked at me uneasily. He was not satisfied with this explanation and thought that something had happened during the day. He advised me to go to bed without further delay, which I readily did.

I felt humiliated at having made an emotional scene, all the more as I was unaware why I had cried. Was it due to pleasure or to crossness? I could not say, and I fell asleep reflecting that it was useless to try and analyse my feeling.

During the ensuing month I devoured the greater number of Walter Scott's works. Since then I have certainly experienced deep and intense joys, but, however great they have been, I do not know if they far exceeded in brightness those which I felt whilst my soul emerged from its mist, like a butterfly from its chrysalis. I proceeded from delight to delight, from one ecstasy to another. I forgot everything, in order to think exclusively of my novels and of the individuals who fired my imagination.

When the Curé explained a problem, I thought of Rebecca, whom I had left in close conversation with the Knight Templar; when he was giving me a history course, I saw marching before me those delightful heroes, from whom my fickle heart had already chosen some fifteen husbands; when he reproached me, I did not hear half his reproofs, being busy making a dress resembling one belonging to Elizabeth of England or Amy Robsart.

'What have you done to-day?' he inquired on arrival.

'Nothing.'

'What do you mean, nothing?'

'That kind of thing bores me,' I said in a tired manner.

The poor Curé was dismayed. He prepared long lectures and delivered them all in one breath; he would, however, have produced just as much effect by addressing a Red Indian.

At length I suddenly became very sad. If my aunt stopped beating me, she made up for it by saying disagreeable things to me. She had guessed that I was distressed at being so short. She lost no opportunity of striking at this vulnerable spot, calling me an abortion, and said repeatedly that I was ugly.

A short time previously I thought I was very pretty and I had far more confidence in my opinion than in my aunt's. But on becoming acquainted with Walter Scott's heroines, doubt arose in my mind. They were so beautiful that I grieved to think I must resemble them in order to be loved.

Out of sympathy, the Curé lost his smiles and his colour. He looked at me in a state of distress, spent his time taking snuff, forgetting all the rules of the art, tried to guess my secret and employed Machiavellian methods to attain his object; but I was inscrutable.

One day I saw him going towards the library, but I knew better than to forget the key in the lock; he retraced his steps, shaking his head and passing his hand through his hair which, in more disorder than ever, produced the effect of a bunch of feathers.

I had hidden behind a door and, when he was near me, I heard him murmur: 'I shall come back with the key!'

This decision annoyed me very much. I told myself that he would certainly discover my secret and that I should not be able to continue my beloved reading.

I immediately went to find several novels, which I carried away to my room, and replaced them on the shelves by books taken at random; despite my precautions, however, I thought that the square of paper, which I had used to replace the broken pane of glass, was a clue which might definitely point to me.

It was on this day that, examining some letters found in the bureau, I discovered my aunt's origin. This furnished me with a weapon against her and I resolved not to delay making use of it.

At lunch the next day she was in a very bad humour. In this state of mind, if she could find no excuse for being unkind to me, she made one up.

I was dreaming of that amiable Buckingham, who appeared adorable in my eyes, with his insolence, his fine clothes, his bows and his intelligence, and I asked myself why Alice Bridgeworth was in despair at finding herself under his roof, when my aunt said to me without preamble: 'How ugly you are this morning, Reine!'

I leapt up from my chair.

'There you are!' I said, passing her the salt-cellar.

'I am not asking for the salt, silly girl! As a matter of fact, you are becoming as stupid as you are ugly!'

I must point out that my aunt never called me *thou* (*tu*). From the day she married my uncle, she thought she rose to the heights of the situation by suppressing the use of *thou* (*le tutoiement*) from her vocabulary. She even called her rabbits *you* (*vous*).

'I do not share your opinion,' I replied dryly. 'I think I am very pretty.'

'What utter nonsense!' exclaimed my aunt. 'Pretty, you? A little abortion, no higher than the fireplace.'

'It is better to resemble a delicate plant than an abortion,' I replied.

My aunt firmly believed that she had been beautiful and failed to understand banter on the subject.

'I was so beautiful, mademoiselle, so beautiful that my sister and I were called goddesses.'

'Was your sister like you, Aunt?'

'Very much; we were twins.'

'Her husband must have been very unhappy,' I said impressively. My aunt uttered an expletive, which I shall not allow my pen to repeat.

'Moreover,' I resumed calmly, 'you naturally have the taste of a woman of the working-classes, whereas I . . .'

I kept my mouth open in the middle of the sentence; my aunt had just broken a plate with the handle of her knife. What I said nullified the efforts she had made until then to conceal her birth from me and afforded me vengeance in full for her unkindnesses to me.

'You are a serpent!' she exclaimed in a choking voice.

'I do not think so, Aunt.'

'A serpent!'

'You have already said so,' I calmly replied, quietly swallowing my last strawberry.

'A serpent warmed in my bosom,' repeated my aunt, who was too angry to use any imagination. I shook my head and told myself that if I were a serpent, I should certainly refuse to find any comfort in that spot.

'Excuse me,' I resumed, 'I have studied that animal in my natural history and I have never noticed that it was in the habit of being warmed in anybody's bosom.'

Invariably disconcerted when I alluded to my reading, my aunt made no reply, but the expression on her face appeared to be so discomforting that I made off, singing out loud:

'There was once an uncle in Le Pavol, Pavol, Pavol!'

It was the middle of June. Butterflies were flying everywhere, flies buzzed, the air was full of a thousand perfumes: in short, the weather seemed so attractive that I forgot my customary caution. I took my book and I went to settle down in a meadow in the shade of a hayrick.

My heart was somewhat heavy as I thought of my aunt's remarks. It is certainly distressing to be too short! Who, then, would ever love me? I consoled myself, however, by reading *Peveril of the Peak*. This was one of the novels of Walter Scott which I liked best, because of Fenella, whose stature was certainly slighter than mine.

I loved and adored Buckingham. I was angry with Fenella, who said things to him which were indeed very unkind and, at the moment when she disappeared through the window, I stopped reading, to exclaim:

'The silly creature! Such a charming man!'

As I said this, I raised my eyes and cried out loudly on seeing the Curé standing before me. With his arms crossed, he looked at me with astonishment. He seemed as amazed as the person in the fairy story who finds his diamonds changed into hazel-nuts. I rose somewhat ashamed, for I had been badly caught.

'Oh! Reine . . .' he began.

'My dear Curé,' I exclaimed, pressing *Peveril of the Peak* to my heart, 'I beg and beseech you, let me continue.'

'Reine, my little Reine, I should never have thought this of you.'

This gentleness touched me all the more, as I never possessed a very clear conscience; but with essentially feminine tact, I hastened to change the subject.

'It was a distraction, Monsieur le Curé, and I was feeling so unhappy.'

'Unhappy, Reine?'

'Do you think it can be amusing to have an aunt like mine? It is true that she no longer beats me, but she says things to me which cause me pain.'

How well I knew my Curé! He had already forgotten his grievances and his reproofs, especially as there was much fundamental truth in my remarks.

'Is that why you are so sad, my dear child?'

'Certainly, Monsieur le Curé. Just think of it, my aunt is always declaring that I am an abortion, that I am frightfully ugly!'

My eyes filled with tears, for this topic went straight to my heart. The worthy Curé, much moved, rubbed his nose perplexedly. He was far from sharing my aunt's views on this point and was wondering what means he had better adopt to dispel my sadness without evoking in my soul pride, vanity and other elements of damnation.

'Come, Reine, you must not attach too much importance to transient things.'

'Still, such things exist,' I replied, my remark coinciding at an interval of two centuries with the thought of the prettiest girl in France.

'And then you will perhaps meet people who do not think like Madame de Lavalle.'

'Are you one of them—Monsieur le Curé? Do you consider me pretty?'

'Well . . . yes,' replied the Curé in a piteous tone.

'Very pretty?'

'Well . . . well, yes,' he replied in the same tone.

'Ah! I am pleased,' I exclaimed, whirling round. 'I do like you, *mon Curé!*'

'That's good, Reine, but you have committed a grievous fault. You entered the library at the risk of breaking your neck, and you have read books which I should probably never have given you.'

'Walter Scott, Monsieur le Curé—Walter Scott; my books speak highly of them.' I told him all my impressions. I talked volubly for a long while, delighted to observe that not only did the Curé no longer think of scolding me, but that he was listening with interest to what I was relating to him. In view of my high spirits and gaiety, which had returned, as if by magic, he suddenly regained his colour and smiles.

'Well, then,' he said, 'I permit you to continue reading Walter Scott; I shall even re-read his works in order to discuss them with you, but promise me not to start your tricks again!'

I promised him gladly and from that time onwards we had a new topic for discussion and arguments, for naturally we were never of the same opinion.

The interest which I took in my novels was, however, wiped out by a sudden and unprecedented event which occurred a few weeks later at 'The Thicket'—one of those events which do not shake empires to their foundations, but which upset the heart and imagination of little girls.

CHAPTER SIX

IT was a Sunday. On Sundays we went regularly to High Mass, the only service held in the morning, the Curé having no Assistant Priest. My aunt led the way to our 'armorial' pew; I followed her, Suzon came next and Perrine came last.

Our little church was ancient and depressing. The primitive colour of the walls was disappearing under a sort of greenish slime, caused by the damp; the floor, far from being level, was made up of gaps and hillocks, which invited the faithful to break their necks and take advantage of their presence in a holy place to reach Heaven sooner; the altar was ornamented with figures of angels painted by the village wheelwright, who prided himself on being an artist; two or three saints looked at one another with surprise, amazed to find they were so ugly. When looking at them on several occasions I told myself that if I were a saint, and if human beings represented me as being so hideous, I should be absolutely deaf to their prayers; but it is possible that saints have not my temperament. Out of a window with a broken pane a white rose reared its scented head and, by its beauty and freshness, seemed to protest against man's bad taste.

We had a harmonium, only three notes of which could be struck; sometimes the number increased to five as the instrument, thanks to the temperature, was subject to whims, like the rheumatism of our lay clerk, who used to roar for two hours with the ingenuous and profound conviction that he had a lovely voice and that it was impossible to resent his having it.

The Celebrant's stool was placed at the edge of a precipice, so that from my pew I only saw the Curé's head and shoulders, which looked penitent. The choir-boys made faces and whispered behind his back, without its occurring to him to get angry.

After the Gospel, he took off his chasuble and stole in front of us, as things were done *en famille*; he stumbled in several holes and reached the pulpit.

Amongst human beings who move about the earth's surface there are none, I assume, who, in the course of their existence, have not had a dream. Be his position in life the lowest or the highest, a man cannot lack desires, and the Curé, subject to civil law, had for thirty years dreamt of possessing a pulpit.

Unfortunately he was badly off, like his parishioners, and my aunt, who was the only person who could assist him, made no reply to his timid hints; besides that, she had a sordid nature when it was a matter of giving something, having the lowest regard for the ambition of her neighbour.

At length, by dint of economizing, the Curé found one day that he possessed two hundred francs. He then resolved that somehow or other he would fulfil his dream.

One morning I saw him arrive out of breath.

'My little Reine, come with me,' he exclaimed.

'Where to, Monsieur le Curé?'

'To church. Come quickly.'

'But Mass is over!'

'Yes, I know; but I have something lovely to show you.'

47

He looked so happy, his worthy face exuded such cheerfulness, that I still laugh when I think of it, and his joy.

He did not walk, he flew, and we arrived at the church, running. The pulpit had just been installed and the Curé, in a state of ecstasy in front of it, said to me in a low voice:

'Look, little Reine, look! Isn't it a blessed invention? At last we have got a pulpit! It doesn't look very substantial, yet it seems firmly made. Now my life dream has been realized. You must never despair of anything, little one, never!'

I looked somewhat surprised, as I could not hide from myself the fact that I had pictured a pulpit as something large and monumental. What I beheld was a sort of wooden box, resting on iron supports which were so low that, if absolutely necessary, one could dispense with steps to enter it. A pulpit without steps, however, does not exist; accordingly, to save one's honour, two steps, each fifteen centimetres high, were successfully placed in position.

'Look, Reine,' said the Curé. 'How good the effect is! When I have a little money, I shall give it a coat of paint; indeed, I shall paint it myself; that will amuse me and will be economical. It certainly could be a little higher, but I must not be too ambitious.'

The poor man walked round the pulpit admiringly. The panels might have been painted by Raphael, or sculptured by Michelangelo: he could hardly have been happier.

He did not reflect that, as always, reality bears little resemblance to a dream. He took care not to make comparisons and enjoyed his happiness without reserve.

'I furnished the design, my little child, and it really was a very good idea. There is, however, an obverse to the medal and I must confess that I have incurred a small debt; the price charged is higher than I supposed, but it appears that that is always the case when a thing is made to order. I reckoned on buying myself a lined great-coat this winter. Well, now I shall have to go without it, that's all!'

As far as I am concerned, his happiness is one of the best memories of that period. I have never seen such a happy man, or one who set off against such a humdrum cheerfulness the reflections of his excellent disposition and his somewhat childish mind.

'It looks just like a pulpit!' he said, smiling and rubbing his hands.

I was rather doubtful on this point, but I hid my deception and did my best to be enraptured at this extraordinary object, which, on account of the irregular shape of the church, was in a recess, so that when the Curé was preaching, three-quarters of the congregation only saw an arm and a lock of white hair, which wagged eloquently, according to the various remarks in the sermon.

The Curé was so happy to say to himself 'I am going into the pulpit' that we had to resign ourselves to having a sermon every Sunday.

Hardly had he opened his mouth than the worthy women in the congregation assumed a comfortable posture, in order to have a little nap, than Perrine profited from the general drowsiness to cast an ogling glance at the pew next to ours, and Reine de Lavalle prepared to reflect on life's vicissitudes, represented by an aunt and the boredom engendered by sermons.

49

I do not know why the Curé liked to expatiate on human passions, but on one occasion, when he was carried away by the warmth of improvisation, I asked him such indiscreet and embarrassing questions at dinner that he vowed never to broach certain subjects when I was present. Thenceforth he merely discussed idleness, drunkenness, anger and other vices, which aroused neither my curiosity nor my chatter.

For an hour he dangled before our eyes the great iniquity into which we had plunged; then, when our state of mind had really become quite distressing, he descended with us into Hell, his face beaming, and made us touch with our fingers the torments which our ravaged souls had merited by sin; after which, passing on with a bold observation to less horrible ideas, he gradually quitted the nether regions, remained for a few moments on earth and finally quietly deposited us in Heaven and descended from the pulpit with the triumphant step of a conqueror who has just cut a Gordian knot.

The congregation then stood with a start, except Suzon, who was too content to hear about the evil of mankind to fall asleep and who used to drink a cup of milk whilst the Curé flogged his flock with his flowery rhetoric.

It was a Sunday. The heat was overwhelming and, on returning to the house, Suzon said:

'There will be a storm before the end of the day.'

This prediction gave me pleasure; a storm was a happy occurrence in my monotonous life and, despite my cowardice, I liked thunder and lightning, although I used to tremble in every limb when the rumbles succeeded one another too rapidly.

During the first part of the afternoon I wandered about the garden and the woods, like a soul in travail.

I was weary to death, telling myself sadly that 1 should never have any adventure and that I was doomed to live with my aunt for ever.

Returning to the house about four o'clock, I went up to the first-floor passage and, with my face glued against a large window-pane, I amused myself by following the movements of the clouds which were gathering above 'The Thicket' and which heralded the storm announced by Suzon.

I asked myself whence they came, what they had seen on their way, what they could relate to me, who knew nothing of life, of the world, and who aspired to see and know things. They had formed behind that horizon which I had never overstepped and which hid me from mysteries, from the splendours (at least, so I thought) of the joys and pleasures on which I inwardly meditated.

I was disturbed in my reflections by observing that Perrine, hidden in a little corner, had allowed herself to be kissed by a hefty rustic, who had put his arm round her waist. I opened the window quickly and, clapping my hands, cried:

'All right, Perrine; I see you, mademoiselle!'

Perrine, frightened, took her sabots in her hand and fled to the stables. The tall rustic took off his hat and regarded me with a silly smile which stretched from ear to ear. I was laughing heartily when a light carriage, whose approach I had not heard, entered the courtyard. A man descended, said something to a servant who accompanied him, and looked around to find someone to whom he could speak.

But Perrine, whose white bonnet I saw peeping through the grilled entrance to the stables, did not stir, and her lover had flung himself flat on his stomach behind a heap of straw. As for me, astounded by this apparition, I pushed open one of the mullions and watched events without making any movement.

The unknown cleared the ramshackle steps in a couple of strides and sought the bell, which had never existed; noticing which, and patience not being his predominant virtue, he vigorously pounded on the door.

My aunt and Suzon arrived together, and I declare that from that moment I had the highest opinion of his courage, for he showed no fear. He made a slight bow and I then understood from his gestures that, the threatening sky having made him uneasy, he asked for shelter at 'The Thicket'.

As a matter of fact, at the same moment the storm broke out with great violence; there was just time to place the carriage and horse under cover.

It is said that solitude begets nervousness; in certain cases, however, it has the opposite effect. Not having provoked anybody, or made any comparisons, I had the greatest confidence in myself and I was completely unaware what exactly constituted this strange feeling, which destroys the most brilliant faculties and renders the most superior man dull.

Nevertheless, confronted with this adventure, which appeared to be the outcome of my thoughts, my heart beat strongly and I hesitated to enter the drawing-room for so long that I was still at the door when the Curé arrived, dripping with rain, but very content.

'Monsieur le Curé,' I exclaimed, darting towards him, 'there is a man in the drawing-room!'

'Well, Reine? A farmer, doubtless?'

'No, Monsieur le Curé, a real man.'

'What do you mean: a real man?'

'I mean that he is neither a Curé nor a peasant; he is young and well-dressed. Let us go in quickly.'

We went in and I nearly uttered a cry of surprise when I noticed that my aunt's expression was really pleasant and that she was smiling agreeably at the unknown person who, sitting opposite her, appeared also at ease, as if he were in his own house.

Yet his looks alone might have sufficed to have cheered the gloomiest soul. He was tall, fairly well-built, with a cheerful face which was frank and open. His fair hair was cut short, his moustache was twisted into points; he had a well-shaped mouth and white teeth, frequently revealed by a frank and natural laugh. His whole being breathed cheerfulness and *joie de vivre*.

On seeing us enter, he rose and waited a moment for my aunt to introduce us. This ceremony was, however, as unknown to her as the inhabitants of Greenland and he introduced himself as Paul de Conprat.

'De Conprat!' exclaimed the Curé. 'Are you the son of that delightful Major de Conprat, whom I used to know?'

'Yes; my father was a major, Monsieur le Curé. Did you know him?'

'He rendered me a service many years ago. What a gallant and delightful man he was!'

'I know that everyone likes my father,' replied M. de Conprat, his face more cheerful than ever. 'It is always a fresh pleasure for me to say so.'

'But are you not a relative of M. de Pavol?' resumed the Curé.

'Yes; I am his third cousin.'

'This is his niece,' said the Curé, introducing me.

Despite my lack of experience, I definitely noticed

that M. de Conprat's look expressed a certain amount of admiration.

'I am delighted to make the acquaintance of such a charming cousin,' he said to me in convincing tones, holding out his hand.

This compliment gave me a pleasant little thrill and I took his hand without any embarrassment.

'Not exactly cousins,' said the Curé, taking snuff delightedly. 'M. de Pavol is only Reine's uncle by marriage; his wife was a Mademoiselle de Lavalle.'

'That doesn't matter,' exclaimed M. de Conprat. 'I do not renounce our relationship. Furthermore, if a good search were made, there would be traces of marriages between my family and that of de Lavalle.'

We began to converse like three old friends and it seemed to me that we had always known and liked each other. I experienced that strange feeling which makes one suppose that what happens just before one's eyes is already in the distant past, so distant that only a vague and almost effaced memory has been retained.

I recalled in vain, however, all the heroes of the novels I knew; I did not find a single one as stout as my very own hero. Without a shadow of doubt, he was a hefty fellow, but he was so good, cheerful and intellectual that this physical defect was promptly transformed in my estimation into an unsurpassed virtue. Soon even my imaginary heroes appeared to me to be devoid of attraction. In spite of their elegant and ever slender figures, they were outclassed, fundamentally outclassed by this fine, well-built boy, who was so vivacious and so intensely cheerful, and whom I mentally endowed with a host of virtues.

Nevertheless, although the storm had diminished in

violence, the rain continued and, as dinner-time approached, my aunt invited Paul de Conprat to dine with us. He immediately declared that he was as hungry as a cannibal and accepted with a cordiality which entranced me.

I slipped away for a moment to face Suzon's ill-temper.

'Suzon,' I said as I entered the kitchen excitedly, 'M. de Conprat is dining with us. Have we got a large capon, some milk, strawberries and cherries?'

'Goodness me, what a business!' grumbled Suzon. 'There is what there is and that's that!'

'Quite so, Suzon! But answer me. Will one capon be insufficient?'

'It is not a question of a capon, but of a turkey; half a minute!'

And Suzon, with a quick movement of pride, opened the oven and made me admire the bird, which, well fattened by her and Perrine, weighed at least twelve pounds; the brown skin was raised in places, thus proving the delicacy and tenderness of the flesh which it hid, and offering my delighted gaze the most pleasing spectacle.

'Bravo!' I said. 'But the clotted cream, Suzon? Did you succeed? Is there much of it? And the salad; dress it carefully.'

'I usually succeed in what I do, mademoiselle. Besides, this gentleman is neither a prince nor an emperor, presumably. He is a man like anybody else; he will adapt himself to what he is given.'

'A man like anybody else, Suzon?' I said indignantly. 'You have not seen him then?'

'Indeed I have, mademoiselle. I have seen and heard him, I can assure you. Is a Christian allowed to knock with all his might the way he did at the door of a respectable house? After that, fall in love with him if you like!'

I opened my mouth to answer severely, but I stopped cautiously, reflecting that, to have her revenge and annoy me, Suzon would be capable of burning up the turkey.

A few minutes later we went into the dining-room, and I could not forbear casting a sorrowful glance at the dirty, worn-out carpet, which was falling into rags. Furthermore, Suzon had a very peculiar way of laying the table. Three salt-cellars were disporting themselves in the middle of the table by way of centrepiece; the spoons and forks were flung down freely; bottles pursued one another, while a solitary water-jug was so placed that each person at the table had to stretch somewhat to reach it, the table being three times too big. For the first time in my life, I had an intuition that all the laws of symmetry had been broken by Suzon's abnormal taste.

M. de Conprat, however, had one of those happy dispositions which find the best in everything, and he had the faculty of identifying himself with the company in which he found himself. He looked merrily at the table, had his soup without stopping his conversation, complimented Suzon and actually cried out with delight at the appearance of the turkey.

'You must admit, Monsieur le Curé,' he said, 'that life is a happy invention and that Heraclitus was endowed with a strong dose of stupidity.'

'Let us not slander philosophers,' replied the Curé. 'They sometimes have good in them.'

'You are full of benevolence, Monsieur le Curé. If I were the Government, I should discharge stupid people and replace them with philosophers, taking care not to isolate them, so that they could devour one another the better.'

'Who was Heraclitus?' said my aunt.

'An idiot, madame, who spent his time whining. How ridiculous to have that reputation for posterity!'

'Perhaps,' I insinuated, 'he used to live with several aunts; that would have soured his character.'

M. de Conprat looked at me astonished and burst out laughing. The Curé glared at me; my aunt, however, who was busy with the turkey, which she was carving skilfully, I must confess, did not hear.

'History glosses over that in silence, Cousin.'

'In any case,' I resumed, 'beware of attacking the ancients; Monsieur le Curé would pluck out your eyes.'

'Ah! the scoundrels, how they have infuriated me! I have only retained one memory of them; the impositions they have cost me.'

'Excuse me,' said the Curé, making an effort to rescue his friends, who were in the process of getting completely submerged in my opinion. 'Excuse me! You cannot deny certain commendable virtues, certain heroic deeds which . . .'

'Illusions, illusions!' interrupted Paul de Conprat. 'They were unbearable scoundrels and, because they are dead, they are adorned with unbelievable virtues, in order to humiliate those poor living persons who are worthier than they. What an excellent turkey!'

As he talked without ceasing, he ate with unequalled appetite and conviviality. Pieces were piled up on his plate and disappeared with such remarkable speed that the moment came when my aunt, the Curé and I stopped with our forks in the air, looking at him in dumb astonishment.

'I have already warned you,' he said, laughing, 'that I was as hungry as a cannibal, which, moreover, happens to me three hundred and sixty-five times a year.'

'What a lot of money you must spend on food!' exclaimed my aunt, who specialized in seizing on the mercenary side of things and making remarks that were out of place.

'Twenty-three thousand, three hundred and seventy-seven francs, Madame,' replied M. de Conprat very seriously.

'Impossible!' murmured my aunt, astonished.

'You seem perfectly happy, monsieur,' said the Curé, rubbing his hands.

'Am I happy, Monsieur le Curé? Rather! Frankly speaking, is it normal to be unhappy?'

'Yes, sometimes,' replied the Curé, smiling.

'Bosh! Unhappy people are often in that state through their own fault, because they take life the wrong way. Mind you, unhappiness does not exist; it is man's stupidity that exists.'

'That is unhappiness,' replied the Curé.

'Negative enough, *per se*, Monsieur le Curé; and because my neighbour is silly, it does not follow that I should imitate him.'

'You like paradoxes, monsieur?'

'No, I do not; but I am indignant when I notice so many people saddening their existence by morbid imagination. I assume that they do not eat enough, that they live on larks or boiled eggs and unsettle their brains at the same time as their stomachs. I adore life: I think everybody should think it is beautiful and that it has but one defect—that it comes to an end so quickly!'

The turkey, salad and cream had all been eaten up and my aunt looked, with an expression which had lost its affability, at the bird's carcass, on which she had reckoned to feast for several days. We were going to leave the table when Suzon half-opened the door and, poking her head through the aperture, said pertly:

'I have made the coffee. Shall I bring it in?'

'Who gave you permission——?' began my aunt.

'Yes, yes,' I said quickly, interrupting her. 'Bring it in at once.' I could have kissed her for this brainwave, but my aunt disagreed with me. She left the room to argue the matter with Suzon, and we only saw her again in the drawing-room.

'You have a wonderful cook, Cousin,' said Paul de Conprat, sipping his coffee.

'True, but she is such a grumbler.'

'That's a detail.'

'What do you think of my aunt?' I asked confidentially.

'Rather pompous,' replied Monsieur de Conprat, a little embarrassed.

'Pompous? You mean disagreeable?'

'Reine,' muttered the Curé.

'Well, let's discuss another subject, Monsieur le Curé, but I should like to have my cousin's happy disposition and discover a better side to my aunt's nature.'

'Acquire a little practical philosophy, my delightful Cousin, which provides a serious foundation to happiness and is the only philosophy which seems to me common sense.'

'What a pity you are not my aunt; how fond of one another we should have been.'

'As for that, I vouch for it!' he exclaimed, laughing.

'And we should need no philosophy to attain that result. But if you don't mind, I prefer not to change my sex, and to be your uncle.'

'I could not ask for anything better, as I am not like Francis I; I have a pronounced antipathy to women.'

'Really?' he resumed, laughing very heartily. 'You are acquainted with the tastes of Francis I?'

The Curé made a despairing gesture, to which M. de Conprat replied with an expressive wink, which meant: 'Be easy, I understand!' This pantomime made me nervous and I made a violent effort to discover its hidden meaning.

'*A propos* of uncles,' I said, 'do you know M. de Pavol well?'

'Yes, I do. My estate lies a league away from his.'

'And his daughter, what is she like?'

'I often played with her when she was a child; but for four years I have lost sight of her. They say she is very beautiful.'

'How much I wish I could be at Le Pavol!' I sighed. 'We should frequently see one another.'

'Who knows, little Cousin? I might not please you if you were better acquainted with me. I can, however, vouch for the fact that I am a worthy fellow; except that I am passionately fond of turkey and I am insanely fond of pretty women, I am not aware that I have even the smallest vice.'

'To like pretty women is not a fault! I myself detest ugly people, such as my aunt, but to compare a turkey to a pretty woman is not very flattering to the latter, Cousin.'

'That is true. I admit that I used an unfortunate expression.'

'I forgive you,' I said quickly. 'So you think I'm pretty?'

For at least two hours I had repeated to myself in my heart of hearts that I must not miss the opportunity of enlightening myself by obtaining straightforward and authoritative advice on a subject teeming with interest to me. Since dinner began I had waited impatiently for the moment to raise my query. Not that I had any doubts as to the answer, but to hear someone, other than the Curé, say point-blank and to your face that you are pretty would be really delightful!

'Pretty, Cousin? You are enchanting! I have never seen such beautiful eyes, or a prettier mouth!'

'What happiness! How pleasant men are, whatever my aunt says about them.'

'Doesn't your aunt like men? She is certainly past the age for flirtation.'

'Flirtation? The subject is never mentioned. Should one flirt?'

'Without a doubt, Cousin; in my estimation it is a great virtue.'

'You haven't taught me that, Monsieur le Curé!' I exclaimed.

During this conversation the unfortunate Curé had a foretaste of the pains of Purgatory. He mopped his face and swallowed his coffee with an effort, apparently finding it full of bitterness.

'Monsieur de Conprat is making fun of you,' he said.

'Are you, Cousin?'

'Not at all,' replied Paul de Conprat, who gave me the impression that he was extremely amused. 'In my opinion, a woman who doesn't flirt is not a woman.'

'All right. I shall try to become one!'

'Let us go into the drawing-room, Mademoiselle de Lavalle,' said the Curé, rising from his chair.

'Good,' I thought. 'The Curé is angry, but I haven't said anything wrong.'

The rain had stopped, the clouds had dispersed and I suggested to Paul de Conprat that we should stroll into the garden. We did so without waiting for permission, followed by the Curé, who looked at us in a manner akin to melancholy, thinking that his beloved lamb was *en route* to perdition.

We ran like children on to the damp grass, getting our feet wet and laughing loudly. We conversed, we chattered, I in particular relating incidents in my life, my petty sorrows, dreams and aversions. What a charming, delightful evening!

M. de Conprat climbed a cherry tree and the violent shaking of the tree caused all the rain on it to descend on me. With his mouth full of cherries and from the top of the tree he remarked that the drops of water were shining in my beautiful hair like a gorgeous ornament, prettier than any he had seen.

'As for Suzon,' I said to myself, 'who makes out that he is a man like any other, is it possible to be so foolish?'

We returned to the drawing-room, where a large fire was lit to dry us. Sitting next to one another, Paul de Conprat and I continued our conversation in mysterious tones.

My aunt, dumbfounded by my audacity, my lack of restraint and the joy which lit up my face, said nothing. The Curé, delighted to find me content, was not so keenly preoccupied that he forgot to make a third party. What an enjoyable evening!

At last M. de Conprat rose to depart and we led him to

the courtyard. He took affectionate leave of the Curé
and thanked my aunt; then, when it came to my turn,
he took my hand and said in a low voice: 'I should have
liked this evening to have lasted for ever, Cousin.'

'So should I; but you will come again, won't you?'

'Certainly, before long, I hope!'

He raised my hand to his lips and human nature must
really have a foundation of great perversity, for this
homage gave me such novel, lively and unmitigated
pleasure that I had the incongruous idea of . . . must I
confess it? Yes, I had the idea, which I did not carry out,
of flinging myself on his neck and kissing him on both
cheeks, in spite of my aunt and in spite of the Curé,
who watched over us like a new kind of dragon, a chubby
and easy-tempered dragon.

CHAPTER SEVEN

AFTER M. de Conprat's departure my state of mind remained for several days in a kind of blessedness, which it would be difficult to describe. I experienced many sensations, which took the outward form of gambols or pirouettes, for the latter, lasting a long time, were my mode of expressing a host of feelings.

When I had whirled about a good deal, I flung myself on to the grass and, with my eyes looking heavenwards, I thought of numerous things, and yet of absolutely nothing. This exquisite moral state, in which the mind lives in a sort of somnolence, a dreamy quietness which resembles sleep, although the mind is very wide awake, has left me with the sweetest memory. From that period dates my foolish passion for the canopy of heaven, which since then has always seemed to me to be in harmony with my thoughts, whether sad or gay, serious or frivolous.

When I had permitted my imagination to wander along shady paths, which were so obscure that it groped in feeling its way, I suffered it to return to the light and dwell upon M. de Conprat. I laughed at the recollection of his frank face, his hearty laugh and his white teeth. I loved the kiss he had imprinted on my hand and I experienced real delight in thinking that, had I followed my line of thought, I could have kissed him on both cheeks. I lingered for a long while on these sweet feelings, until I came to the point of asking myself why my soul was passing through these various phases.

Having arrived at this delicate point, my imagination began to enter the realms of darkness, where it fought against ephemeral ideas, so ephemeral that in despair I abandoned the project, to resume my thoughts of a mouth which pleased me, of eyes which had smiled at me, of an expression which I had firmly decided never to forget.

These strange creatures, my ideas, did not, however, leave me in peace for long and I gradually fell again into their power. I likewise walked in obscurity until, taking it into my head to confirm certain impressions with those of my favourite heroines, light was thrown on one main point.

I discovered that I was in love and that love was the most charming thing in the world. This discovery threw me into transports of the most intense joy. In the first place because my life had been embellished by a charm, which, although vague, was none the less real; next because if I loved, I was certainly loved. As a matter of fact, I loved M. de Conprat because he seemed charming; in consequence, the sight of me must have produced the same havoc in his heart, since he thought I was delightful. My logic, increased by total lack of experience, went no further and was only sufficient to settle my argument and make me happy.

One discovery leads to another and I was led to reflect that charity could only play a very unobtrusive rôle in the sympathy which Francis I felt for women in general and for Anne de Pisseleu in particular; that love bore no resemblance to affection, since I adored the Curé and yet I never wanted to kiss him, whereas I needed no urging to fall on the neck of Paul de Conprat; that it was most ridiculous to adopt a mysterious voice and subterfuges in order to discuss something so natural, on which it was obvious there fell no shadow of evil.

'But a Curé,' I reflected, 'must have erroneous and extraordinary ideas about love, seeing that, as he cannot marry, he cannot love. Francis I was married, however, and . . . I cannot understand that at all, and I must find out.'

There was such chaos in my thoughts that, in spite of my disdainful prejudices regarding the Curé's opinions, I resolved to broach this difficult subject with him.

The poor Curé was perfectly aware that my mind was greatly troubled, but he had too much delicacy and common sense to seem to attach importance to impressions which a confidence might have put a name to. He endeavoured to put me off the track by all the means in his power and, adopting the expedient of coming every day to 'The Thicket', he prolonged the lesson indefinitely.

We were sitting at our window; my aunt, who had been in pain for some time, had retired to her room; I wandered about in the moonlight and the Curé struggled to explain my problems to me.

'See what you have done, Reine! You have worked it out in kilogrammes, instead of in grammes. And here, if three-fifths are multiplied by . . .'

'Monsieur le Curé,' I said, 'guess what is the most delightful thing in the world.'

'What is it then, Reine?'

'Love, Monsieur le Curé.'

'What are you talking about, little one?' exclaimed the Curé uneasily.

'Oh! about something I know very well,' I replied,

shaking my head with a knowing air. 'I even ask myself why you haven't said a word about it, since it can be witnessed every day.'

'That is what comes of reading novels, mademoiselle; you take seriously what is merely imaginary.'

'It is wrong to slander your own thought, Monsieur le Curé! You know that one does love and that it is wholly delightful.'

'That is a subject which does not concern young girls, Reine. You must not talk about it.'

'How can you make out that it does not concern young girls, seeing that it is they who love and are loved?'

'How unfortunate I am,' exclaimed the Curé, 'to have to deal with such a head!'

'Don't speak adversely about my head; I like it very much, especially as M. de Conprat thinks my face is pretty.'

'M. de Conprat made fun of you, Reine. Rest assured, he took you for a little girl of no consequence.'

'Not at all,' I replied, 'for he kissed my hand. And do you know what my idea was at that moment?'

'Well?' replied the Curé, who was on tenterhooks.

'Well, Monsieur le Curé, I was about to fling myself on to his neck.'

'What stupidity! You don't do that when you are unacquainted with the person concerned.'

'Quite so, but he . . . And then, if he had been a woman, I should certainly not have had that idea.'

'Why, Reine, you are talking nonsense.'

'Oh! because . . .'

Silence followed this downright reply and I looked slyly at the Curé, who joggled about and took snuff, to give himself an air of importance.

'My dear Curé,' I said in an insinuating tone, 'if you would be very kind . . .'

'What else, Reine?'

'Well, I want to ask you a few simple questions on subjects which are running through my brain.'

The Curé sank into his armchair like a man who suddenly takes an important step.

'Well, Reine, I am listening to you. It is better to speak openly of what is in your mind than to rack your brains and be incoherent.'

'I am not racking my brains, Monsieur le Curé, nor am I incoherent; only I think of love a good deal, because . . .'

'Because?'

'Nothing. To begin with, tell me how it comes about that, if you were to kiss my hand, I should think it ridiculous and not very pleasant, although I like you with all my heart, whereas it is just the opposite when it is a question of M. de Conprat.'

'What is that? What are you saying, Reine?'

'I am saying that I found it very pleasant that M. de Conprat should kiss my hand, whereas had it been you...'

'But, *ma petite*, your question is ridiculous and the feeling you describe is of no significance and is not worth bothering about.'

'Ah! . . . That is not my opinion. I often think of it and this is what I have discovered; if M. de Conprat's action appeared to give me pleasure, it is because he is young and could be my husband, whereas you are elderly and a priest can never marry.'

'Yes, that is so,' the Curé replied mechanically.

'One always loves one's husband out of love, you will agree?'

'Doubtless.'

'Now, Monsieur le Curé, tell me if it be true that men are known sometimes to love several women.'

'I know nothing about it,' said the Curé, irritated.

'Yes, you must know about it. After all, a husband loves a woman other than his wife, since Francis I loved Anne de Pisseleu and he was married.'

'Francis I was a bad lot,' exclaimed the Curé, exasperated, 'and Buckingham, whom you like so much, was one too!'

'My goodness!' I continued. 'Everybody has a character and I do not see why they were charged with crime for loving several women. Perhaps Queen Claude and Madame Buckingham were like my aunt. Besides, I have just discovered that feelings cannot be controlled and that they can no more refrain from loving than I myself . . .'

'What, Reine?'

'Nothing, Monsieur le Curé. But I am afraid I have a weak spot for bad lots, for Buckingham is very charming!'

'Really, *ma petite*, I have endeavoured to make you understand certain things since you have read Walter Scott, and in my opinion you appear to have understood absolutely nothing.'

'Listen, my dear Curé. Your explanations are not very clear and so much in my head is hazy. All that is very peculiar,' I continued dreamily. 'Well, explain to me why love arouses your indignation.'

'Reine,' said the Curé, beside himself, 'that is enough of the matter. You have such a way of asking questions that it is impossible to give you the answers. I tell you in all seriousness there are subjects you must not mention, and which you cannot understand, because you are too young.'

The Curé put his hat under his arm and fled. I went to the door and shouted: 'You can say what you like, my dear Curé, but I am well informed about love; it is the most delightful thing in the world. *Vive l'amour!*'

Two days went by without the Curé coming to 'The Thicket', so that, distressed at having teased him, I wended my way to the Presbytery on the third day to make a courteous apology. I found him in his kitchen with a meagre lunch, which he was devouring with heartiness and a great appetite.

'Monsieur le Curé,' I said in a comparatively humble tone, 'you are angry?'

'Somewhat, little Reine. You never wish to listen to me.'

'I promise you to stop talking about love, Monsieur le Curé.'

'Above all, Reine, try not to think of things which you don't understand.'

'Oh, which I don't understand! . . .' I exclaimed, at once getting angry. 'I understand very well and, in spite of all the Curés in the world, I shall maintain that . . .'

'Come,' interrupted the Curé, discouraged, 'you are already in the wrong.'

'That's true, my dear Curé, but I assure you that a Curé does not understand anything about it.'

'Neither does Reine de Lavalle. I am going to give you a lesson to-day, my little girl.'

Thus ended the most serious quarrel I had ever had with the Curé.

Days went by; however, Paul de Conprat did not pay a return visit, and my nervous system was shaken and I became ominously peevish. A month after the memorable adventure I had lost my hopes and peace of mind which, added to boredom, plunged me into a state of dreary sadness. It was at that time that the Curé quarrelled with my aunt, who showed him the door. Sitting under the drawing-room window, I heard the following conversation:

'Madame,' said the Curé, 'I have come to discuss Reine with you.'

'For what reason?'

'The child is bored, madame. M. de Conprat's visit has revealed to her mind horizons already made clear by the few novels which she has read. She needs distraction.'

'Distraction! Where am I to take her? I cannot move. I am not well.'

'Then I cannot depend upon you, madame, to distract her. You must write to M. de Pavol and request him to take Reine under his roof for a time.'

'Write to M. de Pavol? Certainly not! The child would not want to return here.'

'That is possible, but that is a secondary consideration, which will be dealt with later. After all, she is called upon to live in the world one day or another and I consider it necessary for her to change her *modus vivendi* and see many things she knows nothing about.'

'I don't agree, Monsieur le Curé. Reine will not leave here.'

'But, madame,' continued the Curé, who was getting annoyed, 'I tell you again that the matter is urgent. Reine is depressed, her intelligence is lively and much exercised. I am sure she imagines that she has fallen in love with M. de Conprat.'

'I don't care,' said my aunt, who was quite incapable of understanding the Curé's arguments.

'There is a quotation, "Loneliness is the devil's advocate", and in the case of young people it is perfectly true. Solitude is bad for Reine; a little distraction would make her forget what, in short, is only childishness.'

'A Curé has funny ideas,' I thought, 'treating lightly a matter so serious and imagining that one day I shall forget M. de Conprat!'

'Monsieur le Curé,' continued my aunt in her crossest voice, 'mind your own business. I shall have my own way; you shan't have yours.'

'Madame, I love that child whole-heartedly and I do not intend that she should be unhappy,' replied the Curé in a tone I did not recognize as his. 'You have buried her at "The Thicket", you have never given her cause for the least satisfaction, and I may say that but for me she would have grown up ignorant and stupid and she might have been a little withered wild flower. I repeat, you must write to M. de Pavol.'

'That is going too far,' exclaimed my aunt indignantly. 'Am I not mistress in my own house? Leave here, Monsieur le Curé, and do not set foot here again.'

'All right, madame. I know now what I have to do and to-day I see clearly that, if I have not taken action earlier, it is because I have been blinded by the selfish pleasure of seeing my little Reine constantly.'

The Curé found me weeping in the avenue.

'Is it possible? Shown the door because of me!' I said. 'What is to become of us if we see no more of each other?'

'You heard the conversation, *ma petite*?'

'Yes, yes, I was beneath the window. Ah! what a woman, what a . . .'

'Come, be calm, Reine,' continued the Curé, who was

blushing and quaking. 'This very evening I shall write to your uncle.'

'Write quickly, my dear Curé. I only hope he comes for me immediately.'

'Let us hope so,' replied the Curé with a sad little smile. Various tasks, however, prevented his writing that evening to M. de Pavol and on the next day my aunt, who had struggled with indisposition for several weeks, fell dangerously ill. Five days later death knocked at the door of 'The Thicket' and changed the course of my life.

CHAPTER EIGHT

IMMEDIATELY after the death of my aunt I took refuge in the Presbytery. My aunt, whom Suzon nursed with great devotion, did not ask to see me once during her illness.

The Curé had written to M. de Pavol to notify him that Madame de Lavalle was ill, but the progress of the illness was so rapid that my uncle received the telegram announcing the fatal *dénouement* before he was able to reply to the Curé's letter. He at once telegraphed to inform us that he would be unable to be present at the funeral service.

The next day we received a letter in which he stated that, not having recovered from an attack of gout, he would not come to 'The Thicket'. He requested the Curé to take me to C—— a few days later, in the hope that he would be sufficiently well to fetch me from there.

My aunt was buried without pomp and ceremony. She was not liked, and started on her journey to the next world without a large *cortège* of sympathy.

I returned from the interment and made a great effort to feel a little sorrow, but did not succeed. Whatever remonstrances my conscience made, I felt only liberation in my brain and my heart. If I had known the *dictum* of a well-known man, I should certainly have applied it to myself and should have exclaimed in a superb fit of misanthropy: 'I do not know what is happening in the mind of a wretched being, but I do know what an honest little girl feels and that frightens me'!

But as I had absolutely no knowledge of that *dictum*, I

could not make use of it to satisfy the shades of my aunt.

My uncle had arranged the date of my departure: August 10th. It was now the 8th and I spent those two days with the Curé, whose worthy countenance grew hourly longer at the thought of our separation.

On Tuesday morning he had an excellent lunch prepared for me and for the last time we sat opposite one another in an endeavour to gain strength. But every mouthful choked us and I had the greatest difficulty in holding back my tears.

The poor Curé got no sleep that night. He was too sad to sleep and, moreover, being unable to accompany me to C——, he had written my uncle a letter of seventeen pages in which, as I discovered later, he enumerated my good points, small, great and middling. There was no question of my failings.

'My dear little child,' he said after a long silence, 'you will not forget your old Curé?'

'Never, never,' I said exuberantly.

'Nor will you forget my advice. Beware of imagination, little Reine. I may compare it to a lovely flame, which lights up and animates the mind when it is fostered discreetly; but if it be overdone, it becomes a bonfire, which sets fire to the house, and the conflagration leaves ashes and dross behind it.'

'I shall strive to control the flame with discretion, Monsieur le Curé, but I confess that I am pretty fond of bonfires.'

'Yes, but beware of fire! Don't play with fire, Reine.'

'Just a little bonfire is delightful, Monsieur le Curé, and if you are afraid of fire, you throw a little cold water on the hearth.'

'But where do you find cold water, *ma petite*?'

'Ah! I don't know anything about it yet, but perhaps I shall find out one day.'

'Pray God you will not,' exclaimed the Curé. 'Cold water, my dear little child, means disillusions and sorrows, and every day I shall pray fervently that they may not obstruct your path.'

Tears overcame me as I listened to the Curé speaking in that strain, and I drank a large glass of water to calm my emotion.

'Before leaving you,' I continued, 'I ought to warn you. I believe that my taste for flirtation is very pronounced.'

'That is the weak spot in all women, I know,' said the Curé, smiling, 'but a little is sufficient, Reine. Besides, mixing with the world will teach you to balance your feelings, and your uncle, moreover, will know how to guide you skilfully.'

'The world must be delightful, Monsieur le Curé, and I am sure to please, as I am so pretty . . .'

'Doubtless, but do not trust exaggerated compliments; beware of vanity.'

'Bah! it is natural to please others: there is no harm in it.'

'Hum, that is rather a cowardly moral standpoint,' replied the Curé, ruffling his hair. 'After all, these arguments belong to your generation and, thank God, you are not yet at the stage of saying with Ecclesiastes: "Vanity of vanities; all is vanity!"'

'How Ecclesiastes exaggerates! And then he is so old. I imagine his ideas must be out of date.'

'Come, let us leave that point. I am well aware that Holy Writ and the thoughts of a poor country clergyman cannot be understood by a pretty young girl, who appears to be somewhat in love with her face.' He looked at me, smiling, but his lips trembled, for the hour of departure was approaching.

'Take care you don't get cold *en route*, Reine.'

'But, Monsieur le Curé, this is August and I am boiled!'

'That is true,' replied the Curé, who was slightly losing his head. 'Then do not put too much on, for fear of catching cold.' We rose after making vain efforts to nibble a few crumbs of bread and a *pâté*.

'I am so sad,' I exclaimed, suddenly bursting into tears, 'sad at leaving you, my dear Curé.'

'Let us not weep; it is quite ridiculous,' said the Curé, without noticing that large tears were trickling down his cheeks.

'Ah!' I continued, seized with sudden remorse, 'I have made you very angry.'

'No, no, you have been the joy of my life, my entire happiness.'

'What will become of you without me, my poor Curé?'

The Curé did not reply. He took a few strides across the room, blew his nose loudly and succeeded in mastering his emotion, which, catching his throat, only took the form of a few sobs.

The jaunting-car was at the door. Perrine, in all her finery, was to accompany me to C—— and hand me over to my uncle. The farmer was instructed to take us instead of Suzon, who, to her utmost mortification, was to remain for the time being as caretaker at 'The Thicket'.

I told Jean to go ahead and the Curé and I walked a little way, in order to be together a while longer.

'I shall write to you every day, Monsieur le Curé.'

'I do not ask for as much as that, my dear child. Just write to me once a month and write intimately.'

'I shall write to you about everything, absolutely everything, even my ideas on the subject of love.'

'We shall see about that,' said the Curé with an incredulous smile. 'Your future life will be such a novelty to you, filled with so many distractions, that I do not rely very much on your punctuality.'

Jean had waited for us and I saw that I had better depart. I seized the Curé's hands, weeping bitterly.

'Life has very unpleasant moments, Monsieur le Curé!'

'They will pass away,' he replied in a broken voice. 'Adieu, my dear. Do not forget me, and be on your guard . . .'

He could not finish his remark, however, and hurriedly assisted me into the carriage. I took my aunt's old seat, crushed on one side by a trunk without any lock, and on the other by numerous packages of the most weird shape, done up by Perrine.

'Adieu, my old Curé, adieu!' I exclaimed.

He gave an affectionate wave and turned away abruptly. Through my tears I saw him walking away with great strides and putting his hat on, conclusive evidence that his spirits had not only been violently disturbed, but were absolutely topsy-turvy.

After sobbing for quite ten minutes, I thought it time to follow the advice of Perrine, who said in every kind of tone:

'You must be guided by reason, mamselle, be guided by reason.'

I stuffed my handkerchief into my pocket and began reflecting.

Life is indeed a very strange thing. Who would have

believed a fortnight ago that my dreams would be fulfilled so quickly and that I should so soon see M. de
Conprat again? This bewitching idea chased away the
last clouds which overshadowed my mind and I began
to reflect that the heavens were beautiful, life was sweet
and that aunts who go to heaven or hell are endowed
with superior judgment.

My second thought was for my uncle. I was extremely
uneasy as to the impression I should make on him, and I
was conscious that the black dress and the peculiar hat
Suzon had dressed me in made me look a ridiculous
fright. This wretched hat was really torturing me,
mentally torturing me. Trimmed with crêpe, and dating
from the death of M. de Lavalle, it looked like a ship's
biscuit, which bold snails would have chosen for the scene
of their diversions. It evidently made me look hideous
and, this idea being unendurable, I took off my hat and
packed it into my pocket, the size and depth of which
were an honour to Suzon's practical genius.

I was next tormented by the fear of appearing stupid,
for I knew that many things which seemed natural to
everybody would be a source of surprise and admiration
to me. I therefore resolved, in order to avoid letting my
self-respect be in peril of mockery, to hide my astonishment carefully.

These various anxieties prevented my finding the
journey long and I thought I was still a long way from
C—— when we were nearly there. We went straight to
the station, after crossing the town as rapidly as the stiff
legs of our horse permitted.

My uncle was neither tall nor thin; I had naturally
pictured him as sparsely built and tall. I was therefore
astonished when I saw an old fellow with ponderous

gait approach the carriage and exclaim—supposing my uncle ever did such a thing:

'How do you do? I really thought I should have to wait.'

He gave me his hand to get out of the carriage and kissed me cordially. After which, examining me from head to foot, he said:

'No higher than an elf, but devilishly pretty!'

'That is my opinion, Uncle,' I replied, modestly lowering my eyes.

'Ah! you think so too?'

'Rather, and the Curé agrees, and so does . . . But here is a letter for you from the Curé, Uncle.'

'Why isn't he here?'

'He has been detained, because of various religious services.'

'What a pity! I should have been pleased to see him. Has my niece no hat?'

'Yes, Uncle. It is in my pocket.'

'In your pocket? Why?'

'Because it is hideous.'

'That's a fine reason! Does one ever carry a hat in one's pocket? You can't travel without a hat, *ma petite*. Hurry up and put your hat on whilst I have your luggage registered.'

Somewhat disconcerted by this attack, I replaced my hat on my head, not without observing that a journey in one's pocket was certainly not good for that specimen of human industry.

I then said goodbye to Jean and Perrine.

'Ah! mamselle,' said Perrine, 'even if you were a good, fine cow I should not be more sorry to part from you.'

'Many thanks,' I said, half laughing, half crying. 'Let us kiss and say goodbye.'

I kissed Perrine's firm, rosy cheeks, on which, I fear, more than one wretch, talking in dulcet tones, had implanted a few furtive or resounding kisses.

'Adieu, Jean.'

'*Au revoir*, mamselle,' said Jean, laughing inanely, somehow or other showing emotion.

A few minutes later I was in the train, facing my uncle, absolutely scared by the commotion at the station and the novelty of my position. When I felt a little better, I looked at M. de Pavol.

My uncle, of medium height, squarely built with broad shoulders, large, red, badly kept hands, hardly gave the impression, at first glance, of having an aristocratic appearance. His face was ruddy, his forehead large, nose prominent, his hair cut very short in tufts, his eyes were small, searching and deeply set beneath bushy, pro-tuberant eyebrows. But beneath this common exterior, the man of the world and of breeding was promptly noticeable. The outstanding feature of his face, which struck me most, was his mouth. It was firm, vigorous, and rather fine-looking, although the lower lip was somewhat thick; this mouth had a fine, ironical, derisive, cunning, teasing expression, which baffled the less timid and riveted their attention. In studying him, you completely forgot the commonness which my uncle's physique exhibited or, to express it more clearly, you found no more common traits in him and agreed that his artless nature was a frame which admirably displayed this intellectual mouth.

My uncle did not talk much and, when he did so, it was slowly, but that little generally bore weight. He sometimes chose to use lively expressions, which produced an effect all the greater because they were expressed slowly and sedately. He was just over sixty years of age; nevertheless, as he was subject to frequent attacks of gout, his spirits were rather depressed by physical suffering. But if he no longer indulged in lively repartee as in former times, his mouth, by a movement often barely perceptible, expressed all the *nuances* which exist in irony, finesse, open or teasing mockery, and I have seen my uncle pulverize people before he even uttered a word.

I was naturally too lacking in experience to make an immediate and profound study of M. de Pavol, but I looked at him with the greatest interest. On his part, whilst reading the letter which I had brought with me, he looked at me attentively from time to time, as if to establish the fact that my features did not belie the Curé's statements.

'You are looking very intently at me,' he said. 'Am I by chance handsome, in your opinion?'

'Not in the least.'

My uncle made a slight grimace.

'That's frank, or I am no judge of such things. Could you tell me why you are so pale?'

'Because I am dying of fright, Uncle.'

'Afraid of whom?'

'We are going so fast, it is terrifying!'

'I understand perfectly. It is the first time you have travelled. Rest assured there is no danger.'

'And my cousin, Uncle, is she at Le Pavol?'

'Yes; she is delighted to be making your acquaintance.'

My uncle asked me a few questions about my aunt and

my life at 'The Thicket'; he then picked up a newspaper and remained silent until our arrival at V——.

We then entered a two-horsed landau, which was to take us to Le Pavol. My bulky parcels were piled up somehow in this elegant carriage and they cut a shabby figure, which humiliated me profoundly. We had hardly taken our seats before my uncle gave me a bag of cakes to cheer me up again, and started reading another newspaper. This way of acting began to annoy me.

It was not in my nature to remain silent for long, and, besides, I had a large number of questions to ask. So when I had had enough of the pleasure of feeling myself transported in a beautiful carriage, which ran well and was well padded, I risked breaking my silence.

'Uncle,' I said, 'if you don't want to read any more, we could have a little chat.'

'With pleasure,' replied my uncle, at once folding up his newspaper. 'I thought you would like to be left to your thoughts. What subject shall we discuss? The Eastern question, political economy, dolls' clothes, or the habits of monkeys?'

'All these interest me little; and as regards the habits of monkeys, I imagine, Uncle, that I know as much as you do about them.'

'Quite possibly,' replied M. de Pavol, rather astonished at my self-possession. 'Well, choose your subject.'

'Tell me, Uncle, are you a bit of a miscreant?'

'What the devil did you say?'

'I am asking you, Uncle, if you are not a bit of a miscreant or bully?'

'Are you making fun of me?' exclaimed my uncle, in a tone which was not very civil.

'Don't get angry, Uncle. It is a study of customs which

I am starting, more interesting than that relating to monkeys. I want to know if my aunt was right: she maintained that all men were scoundrels.'

'Hadn't your aunt any common sense, then?'

'She had plenty when she left for the next world, but otherwise she had none,' I calmly replied.

M. de Pavol looked at me with obvious surprise.

'Really, my dear niece, that is rather a crude way of expressing your thoughts. You did not get on with Madame de Lavalle?'

'Not at all. She was very disagreeable and struck me more than once. Ask Monsieur le Curé, to whom she showed the door, on my account, because he defended my interests. And how is it, Uncle, that you allowed me to remain with her for so long? She was a common woman and you did not like her.'

'When your parents died, Reine, my wife was very ill, and I was only too content for my sister-in-law to take charge of you. I saw you again when you were six years old; you appeared to be cheerful and well looked after, and since then, well . . . I have almost forgotten you. To-day I keenly regret it, as you were not happy.'

'You will always keep me with you now, won't you, Uncle?'

'Certainly,' replied M. de Pavol almost eagerly.

'When I say always . . . I mean until my marriage, for I shall marry soon.'

'You are going to marry soon? Come now, you are hardly out of the nursery and you talk of marrying! Marriage is a silly invention. Get that into your head.'

'Why?'

'Women aren't worth a rap,' replied my uncle in tones of conviction.

Startled, I flung myself back into my corner, thinking that this opinion was not very flattering to my Aunt de Pavol. After pondering on my uncle's remark, I continued:

'But since I shall marry a man, it does not matter to me in the least that women aren't worth a rap. My husband will get on with me, just as he can.'

'There's logic. It seems that you can argue. It is well known that young girls are crazy to marry.'

'Does my cousin share my views then?'

'Yes,' replied my uncle gloomily.

'Ah! all the better,' I said, rubbing my hands. 'Is my cousin tall?'

'Tall and beautiful,' replied M. de Pavol agreeably, 'a real goddess and the apple of my eye. However, you will see her in a moment, for we are nearly there.'

We had indeed turned into an avenue of enormous elms, which led to the *château*.

My cousin was waiting for us on the steps. She held out her arms to me with the majesty of a queen granting a favour to her subjects.

'Goodness, how beautiful you are!' I said, looking at her with astonishment.

It is certainly a rare thing to come across unquestionable beauty, but my cousin's beauty stood out and could not be disputed. She did not always look pleasant, her face being haughty and at times harsh, but even those who admired her least were obliged to exclaim, like my uncle: 'She is devilishly beautiful!'

She had brown hair, arranged low on the forehead, a Greek profile of perfect purity, a superb complexion, and blue eyes with dark eyelashes and well-designed eyebrows. Tall, strong, with a very well-developed

85

bosom, she might have been taken for eighteen years of age if her mouth, despite a rather disdainful bow which threatened to become too accentuated later on, had not displayed childish movements, denoting extreme youth. Her gait and her gestures were slow and rather listless, but they were always harmonious and devoid of affectation. A friend of M. de Pavol said one day, laughingly, that at the age of twenty-five she would resemble Juno in one feature after another. The name of Juno stuck to her.

I suddenly acquired a genuine passion for my lovely cousin, and my uncle was much amused at my astonishment.

'Haven't you ever seen any pretty women?'

'No, I haven't, for I have been buried alive in a hole.'

'You might look at yourself in the glass, Reine; M. de Conprat had told us that you were pretty.'

'Paul de Conprat?' I exclaimed.

'That's right,' continued my uncle. 'I forgot to speak to you about him. It seems that he sheltered at "The Thicket" on a stormy day.'

'I remember it well,' I replied, blushing.

'Will he come to lunch on Monday, Blanche?'

'Yes, Father; the Major wrote to-day, accepting the invitation. Who dressed you, Reine?'

'Suzon, a servant of my aunt's, with bad taste and stupidity,' I replied spitefully.

'From to-morrow onwards we shall remedy what is lacking in your clothes. Only have a little more respect for the memory of Madame de Lavalle. You did not like her, but she has passed away, and peace be to her soul! Come to dinner; Juno will afterwards show you to your rooms.'

I spent part of the night at my window, indulging in delightful dreams and contemplating the gloomy rows of the lofty trees of Le Pavol, where I was to laugh, cry, amuse myself, feel sad and see my destiny fulfilled.

I was so happy that the Curé, on this occasion, was only an imperceptible part of my reflections.

CHAPTER NINE

I DO request, however, that I may not be deemed heartlessly frivolous and inconstant, for this forgetfulness was only transitory and, three days after my arrival at Le Pavol, I wrote the following letter to the Curé:

'MY DEAR CURÉ,—I have so many things to tell you, so many discoveries to describe, so many confidences to make to you, that I do not know where to begin. Just imagine that the sky is more beautiful than at "The Thicket", that the trees are larger, that the flowers are fresher, that everything is pleasant, that an uncle is a happy invention on the part of nature, and that my cousin is as beautiful as a fairy. It would be useless for you to lecture, scold or preach to me, my dear Curé, you will not rid me of the idea that if Francis I loved women as beautiful as Blanche de Pavol, he had very sound judgment. You yourself, Monsieur le Curé, would fall in love with her if you saw her. But I confess that her queenly manners frighten me somewhat—I, whom nothing intimidates. And then she is so tall . . . and I could have wished that she had been short, that might have consoled me, although I now know that my little figure is supple, elegant, and in perfect proportion! It does not matter if I had been a few centimetres taller; what would that have been to God?

'I shall not describe my uncle, because I am aware that you know him, but I can see already that I shall like him and that I have got round him. It is a great happiness to have a pretty face, my dear Curé, much greater than you cared to tell me; one pleases everybody, and when I am a grandmother, I shall relate to my grandchildren that that is the first, delightful discovery that I made when I began my life. But there is time yet to think of it.

'Although I experience surprise after surprise, I have already become perfectly used to Le Pavol and to the luxury all around me. Nevertheless, I should sometimes utter cries of astonishment if I were not afraid of appearing ridiculous; I am concealing my impressions, but I confess to you, my dear Curé, that I am often greatly astonished.

'The day before yesterday we went to V——, in order to buy some clothes, Suzon's "creations" being decidedly ghastly. Let us be under no illusions, my poor Curé, in spite of your admiration for certain dresses; I arrived here looking an awful fright.

'Ah! how pleasant a town is. I am enraptured and astonished at the streets, the shops, the houses and churches, and Blanche has made fun of me, because she calls V—— a "hole on a hill". What is to be said of "The Thicket", then? After spending three hours at the dressmaker's and the milliner's, my cousin, who is very pious, went to confession, and left me with the chamber-maid, to make a few purchases. My uncle had given me some money for useful and practical purchases, but would you believe that I simply cannot determine what constitutes "useful and practical things"? I began by running to the *pâtisserie* and stuffing myself with small cakes; I humbly confess to a passion for small cakes. Whilst I was thus occupied so usefully and pleasantly— you would agree for, after all, it is an important duty to nourish this mean body—I noticed some very pretty things in a shop opposite the *pâtisserie*. I at once went there and bought forty-two little terra-cotta men, all there were in the shop. After that, not only was I without a halfpenny, but I was deeply in debt, which does not matter much, as I am wealthy. My cousin laughed heartily, but my uncle scolded me. He wanted me to understand that common sense must ballast human intelligence, old or young, that it is an excellent virtue at any age and that without it, one acts stupidly. For example: I purchased forty-two terra-cotta men instead of providing myself with stockings and underwear. I listened to this speech with a contrite and humiliated air, my dear Curé, but towards the close, which was certainly very fine, my rebellious spirit gave to common sense an ungraceful body, a long, even a Roman nose, a lean and surly face, and this individual was so like my aunt that, there and then, I took a dislike to common sense. Such was the result of the eloquence displayed by my uncle. In the meantime, I have forty-two old men, crying, smiling, making faces, spread about in my room and I am satisfied.

'Yesterday evening I chatted to Blanche about love. Monsieur le Curé, didn't you tell me that it only existed in books and that it did not concern young girls? . . . Ah! my dear Curé, I am afraid that you have often taken me in. When the early weeks of mourning have gone by, we shall mix with the world. My uncle thinks that I am too young, but I cannot remain alone at Le Pavol. If there had been any question of it, you understand, Monsieur le Curé, there would only be one thing for me to do: either to fling myself out of the window or set fire to the *château*.

'It appears that I have hopes of great success, as I am pretty, and I have a large dowry. Blanche informed me that a pretty face without a dowry is not worth much, but that both together form a perfect *ensemble* and are a "rare dish". I am, therefore, my dear Curé, a savoury, delicate, succulent dish, which will be coveted, sought after and swallowed in the twinkling of an eye, and I very much want to permit it. I shall not permit it, rest assured, unless . . . Mum's the word!

'I await Monday with impatience, Monsieur le Curé, but I shall not tell you why. On that occasion an event will take place which will make my heart beat, an event which makes me want to whirl round until I am out of breath, to throw my hat into the air, to dance, to do stupid things. My goodness, how beautiful life is!

'Nothing is perfect, however, for you are not here and I miss you. I cannot say how much I miss you, my poor Curé. I should so like to make you like the *château* and the well-kept gardens, which are so unlike "The Thicket". I should so like to have you enjoy the easy, comfortable life we lead here. Everything is in order down to the minutest detail, and I verily believe that I am in an earthly Paradise. Every moment there is some new pleasure, or cause for admiration, and every moment I want to tell you about it; I look for you, and call for you, but the echoes of this lovely park remain mute.

'Adieu, my dear Curé. I shall not kiss you, because one does not kiss a Curé (I wonder why not?), but I send you everything my heart possesses and it is full of tenderness. I adore you, Monsieur le Curé.

R EINE.'

Certainly I at once got used to the atmosphere of luxury and elegance into which I had been abruptly plunged. It is equally certain that although Blanche was very nice to me and had decided that we should call each other 'thou', she intimidated me during the first few days after my arrival at Le Pavol. Her attitude of a goddess, her somewhat haughty manner, her idea that she had far more experience than I had, all that obtruded on me and prevented my being very informal with her; but this impression lasted only as long as a white frost in the April sun and, following a conversation which we had in my room on Sunday morning, the fascination with which I regarded her disappeared absolutely.

I was still in bed half dozing, cuddling myself, opening an eye occasionally to look at my cheerful, comfortable room with delight, my little terra-cotta men and the trees which I saw through my open window. Blanche entered my room in a flowing dress, her hair down and looking worried.

'As beautiful as the most beautiful heroines of Walter Scott!' I said, looking at her with admiration.

'Little Reine,' she said, sitting at the foot of my bed, 'I have come to have a chat with you.'

'All the better. But I am not quite awake and my ideas will suffer the effects of it.'

'Even if it be a question of marriage?' continued Blanche, who already knew my opinion of that grave subject.

'Marriage? I am wide awake,' I said, sitting suddenly upright.

'Do you want to marry, Reine?'

'Do I want to marry? . . . What a question! Of course, and the sooner the better. I adore men. I like them much better than women, except when the women are as beautiful as you.'

'You shouldn't say that you adore men,' said Blanche severely.

'Why not?'

'I don't exactly know why, but I assure you that it is not proper for a young girl to do so.'

'All the worse! . . . Besides, that is my opinion,' I replied, pulling the bedclothes over me.

'Child!' said Blanche, looking at me with a sort of pity, which seemed to me rather offensive. 'I came to talk to you about my father, Reine.'

'What about him?'

'Like you, I want to marry some day or other; my father has already refused several offers for me, but I don't care, because I am in no hurry. I shall wait until I am twenty; only I should like to know if he will always oppose my marriage.'

'You must ask him about it.'

'As far as that is concerned,' continued Blanche, a little embarrassed, 'I have to admit that my father frightens me, or rather intimidates me.'

Filled with surprise, I raised myself on my elbow and I removed the hair which was covering my face, so that I could see my cousin better. At that moment she tumbled down from the Olympian clouds on which I had placed her, and beneath Juno's lovely body I discovered a young girl who would never intimidate me any more.

'Nobody intimidates me,' I exclaimed, seizing my pillow and flinging it across the room. Blanche looked at me, astonished.

'What are you doing, Reine?'

'Ah! it is a habit of mine. . . . When I was at "The Thicket" I always threw my pillow about to infuriate Suzon, who was exasperated by this behaviour.'

'As Suzon isn't here, I advise you to give up the habit. To revert to what we were discussing, do you feel brave enough to have a discussion with my father about marriage, which he criticizes unceasingly?'

'Yes; I am very good at having discussions, you will see. By and by I shall tackle my uncle and pursue things vigorously.'

During dinner I made expressive faces at my cousin to tell her that I was about to open hostilities. My uncle, who scented danger, was looking at us under his huge eyebrows, and Blanche, already disconcerted, made a sign to me to remain quiet. But I snapped my fingers, coughed loudly and leapt resolutely into the arena.

'Can one have children if one is unmarried, Uncle?'

'Certainly not,' replied my uncle, apparently amused by my question.

'Would it be a misfortune if humanity were wiped out?'

'Hum! that is a serious question. Philanthropists would answer in the affirmative and misanthropes in the negative.'

'But what is your opinion, Uncle?'

'I haven't thought much about it. However, as I consider that what Providence has done has been done well, I am in favour of the perpetuation of the human species.'

'Then you are inconsistent, Uncle, when you condemn marriage.'

'Ah!' he said.

'As you cannot have children without being married and you are in favour of the propagation of the human race, it follows that you must agree to marriage for everybody.'

'By Jove!' continued M. de Pavol, curling his lip so scornfully that it made Blanche blush. 'That is what is called an argument. What is marriage, in your opinion, my dear niece?'

'Marriage?' I said enthusiastically. 'It is the finest institution on the face of the earth. A perpetual union with the man you love. You sing and dance together and he kisses your hand. Oh! it is delightful.'

'He kisses your hand. Why your hand?'

'Because it is . . . well, that is my idea,' I said, wafting a smile full of mystery to my past.

'Marriage is an institution which delivers the victim to the executioner,' grumbled my uncle.

'Oh!' Juno and I protested vigorously.

'Who is the victim, Father?'

'The man, of course.'

'All the worse for the men,' I replied in decisive tones. 'Let them defend themselves. As for me, I am ready to turn executioner.'

'What are you leading up to now, mesdemoiselles?'

'To this point, Uncle; Blanche and I are devotees of marriage and we have resolved to put our theories into practice. I want it to be as soon as possible.'

'Reine,' cried my cousin, astonished at my audacity.

'I am only telling the truth, Blanche; only you want to wait, but I have no patience.'

'Really, my dear niece. I suppose, however, that you have nobody in mind?'

'Naturally not,' said Blanche, laughing. 'She does not know a soul!'

Since my arrival at Le Pavol I had thought a good deal of my love and of M. de Conprat, and I had asked myself a number of times if I ought to reveal the intimate secret of my heart to my cousin. But upon reflection I decided, under the circumstances, to break all my principles and ally myself with the Arab, who says that silence is golden. However, in the face of Blanche's remark and despite my firm resolution to preserve my secret, I was on the point of divulging it, but I succeeded in overcoming the temptation to speak.

'At any rate I shall fall in love some day or other, for it is impossible to live without love.'

'Really? Where did you get hold of those ideas, Reine?'

'But it's life, Uncle,' I replied quietly. 'Look at the heroines of Walter Scott: how they love and are loved!'

'Ah! was it the Curé who allowed you to read novels, and gave you a course of lectures on love?'

'My poor Curé! How angry I made him about that! As for novels, Uncle, he didn't want to give me any; he even took away the key of the library, but I entered by the window, by breaking a window-pane.'

'That's promising! Afterwards you hastened to dream and rave about love?'

'I never rave, especially on that point, as I am well up in what we are discussing.'

'The devil,' said my uncle, laughing. 'You have just told us, however, that you do not love anybody.'

'Certainly,' I replied eagerly, somewhat confused at my blunder. 'But don't you think that reflection can make up for experience, Uncle?'

'Why, of course! My mind is made up, above all on such a subject. And besides, you appear to be fairly level-headed.'

'I am merely logical, Uncle. Tell me: does one ever love a man who is not one's husband?'

'No, never,' replied M. de Pavol, smiling.

'Well, since that is the case, one is always naturally in love with one's husband and cannot live without loving. I conclude that one ought to marry.'

'Yes; but not until you have reached the age of twenty-one, mesdemoiselles.'

'I don't care,' replied Blanche.

'But in my case I do care very much. I shall never wait five years.'

'You will wait five years, except in exceptional circumstances.'

'What do you call "exceptional circumstances", Uncle?'

'A man, so suitable from every point of view, that it would be ridiculous to refuse him.'

This modification in my uncle's plans gave me such pleasure that I got up and did a pirouette.

'Then I am sure of my case,' I exclaimed, running away. I took refuge in my room, where Juno soon appeared majestically.

'You are brazen-faced, Reine!'

'Brazen-faced? Is that the way you thank me when I did what you wanted me to?'

'Yes; but you express things too straightforwardly.'

'It's my way. I like straightforward things.'

'Besides, one would have thought you wanted to tease my father.'

'I should be distressed if I vexed him; he pleases me with his mocking face and I already like him immensely. But do not let us change the subject, Blanche; it is he who makes us indignant by protesting against marriage, and after all you know what you wished to know.'

'Certainly,' replied Blanche dreamily.

M. de Pavol soon learnt to his cost that if women are not worth a rap, little girls aren't much better and crush the ideas of a father and an uncle under foot without turning a hair.

CHAPTER TEN

O N Monday morning I got up with a feeling of keen
pleasure. During the night I had dreamt of Paul de
Conprat and I woke up with a cry of joy.

The delight of putting on, for the first time, a dress
such as I had never possessed before, added still more to
my joy and, when I had dressed, I looked at myself for a
long time in silent admiration. Then I began to pirouette
in an outburst of exuberant happiness and I nearly
knocked over my uncle in the passage.

'Where are you running to?'

'Into various rooms, Uncle, to see myself in all the
mirrors. Look how fine I am.'

'Not bad, I agree.'

'Doesn't my figure look pretty in a well-made dress?'

'Charming,' replied M. de Pavol. My joy appeared to
fascinate him and he embraced me on both cheeks.

'Oh! how happy I am, Uncle! I think, as Perrine used
to say, that the "exceptional circumstances" will arise soon.'

Thereupon I left him and burst into Juno's room.

'Look,' I cried, turning round so quickly that my
cousin could only perceive a whirling cloud.

'Stay quiet for a while, Reine,' she said with her usual
calmness. 'When will you achieve some poise? Yes;
your dress fits well.'

'Look what a small foot I have got,' I said, stretching
out my leg.

'What innate coquetry!' exclaimed Blanche, laughing.
'Who would have thought that a little thing like you
would have already arrived at such a pitch of coquetry?'

'You will see something quite different,' I answered gravely. 'I am aware, you see, that coquetry is a virtue, a serious virtue.'

'It is the first time I have heard it. Who taught you that? It wasn't the Curé, I suppose?'

'No, no, but someone who understands all about it. Have we any other guests beside the de Conprats, Blanche?'

'Yes; the Curé and two friends of my father.'

We made ourselves comfortable in the drawing-room, waiting for our guests, and soon my uncle arrived, accompanied by Major de Conprat, to whom he introduced me.

Goodness, what a fine face the Major had!

His eyes were as clear as a child's, with a moustache and hair white as snow; his features were so fine, so benevolent, that he recalled my Curé, although there could be no real resemblance between them. I at once felt drawn towards him, and I noticed that the sympathy was mutual.

'A little relative of whom I have heard,' he said, taking my hands. 'Permit me to kiss you, my child. I was a friend of your father's.'

I let him kiss me with a good grace, not without saying to myself that it would be far preferable for his son to replace him in this delicate operation.

At last he came in . . . and I would gladly have exchanged my whole dowry and my pretty dress into the bargain for the right to run to him and fling my arms around him. He shook hands with my cousin and greeted me so formally that I remained speechless.

'Give me your hand,' I said. 'You know perfectly well that we know one another.'

'I was awaiting your pleasure, mademoiselle.'

'How stupid!'

'Come, Reine,' rebuked my uncle.

'A somewhat wild flower,' said the Major, looking at me in a friendly manner, 'but certainly a pretty flower!'

These remarks did not succeed in dispelling the annoyance which 1 felt without knowing, any too well, why, and I remained silent for some time in my corner, looking at M. de Conprat, who was chatting gaily to Blanche. Oh! how I liked him! How my heart beat when I heard again that fine laugh, saw those white teeth and those candid eyes, of which I had dreamed so much in my horrible old home. And my aunt, the Curé, Suzon, the bedewed garden, the cherry-tree which he had climbed, filed past in my memory like transient shadows.

Shortly afterwards I joined in the conversation, and I had recovered a measure of my good humour when we went into the dining-room.

Sitting between the Curé and M. de Conprat, I immediately attacked the latter.

'Why didn't you return to "The Thicket"?' 1 said.

'I was not free of engagements, Cousin.'

'Was that at least a matter of regret?'

'Great regret, 1 assure you.'

'Why, then, did you not give me your hand on arrival?'

'It was for you to do so, mademoiselle, according to etiquette.'

'Oh, etiquette! You did not think of that before.'

'We were living under special conditions and were certainly far from Society,' he replied, smiling.

'Does the world prevent you from being agreeable?'

'Well, not exactly; only convention often suppresses the warmth of friendship.'

'How very silly,' I said briefly.

I was, however, sufficiently satisfied with the explanation to regain all my high spirits. Nevertheless, I noticed, when chatting to him, that he did not attach the same importance as I did to the remarks he had made to me at 'The Thicket'. But I was so delighted to see him, to talk to him that at the time this little deception made little impression on my mind and caused me no misgivings.

M. de Conprat informed us that there would be several balls in the month of October.

'I am delighted to hear it,' replied Juno.

'You will teach me how to dance,' I said, leaping up from my chair.

'I beg you to appoint me your professor,' exclaimed Paul de Conprat.

'Paul is an accomplished waltzer,' said the Major; 'all the women want to waltz with him.'

'And besides, he is charming!' I replied impressively.

The Major and his son began to laugh; the Curé and my uncle's two friends looked at me, smiling and shaking their heads in a paternal way. But the face of M. de Pavol assumed a discontented expression and my cousin raised her eyebrows in an action peculiar to her when something displeased her, a movement full of such disdain that I had the painful feeling that I had said something silly.

After lunch we wandered about the woods; I had recovered my cheerfulness and I talked without ceasing, amusing myself by mimicking the figure and accent of one of our guests, the ridiculous aspects of which had struck me.

'Reine, how ill-bred you are,' said Blanche.

'That is how he talks,' I replied, pinching my nose in order to imitate the voice of my victim.

And M. de Conprat laughed; but Juno enveloped herself in an imposing dignity, which did not trouble me in the least. The moment came when I found myself near him, whilst my cousin walked ahead of us with a nonchalant air. I observed that he was looking at her a good deal.

'She is beautiful, isn't she?' I said in the innocence of my heart.

'Beautiful, very beautiful,' he replied in a contented voice which made me tremble.

Doubt and foreboding crossed my mind; but at the age of sixteen that kind of impression takes flight and disappears like the butterflies which fly around us, and I was madly gay until the moment when our guests took leave of M. de Pavol.

When they had departed, my uncle went to his study and summoned me to him.

'Reine, you have been ridiculous.'

'How is that, Uncle?'

'You don't say to a young man that he is charming, my dear niece.'

'But I think he is, Uncle.'

'All the more reason for not saying so.'

'I do not understand you,' I replied, nonplussed. 'Then I ought to have said that I found him the reverse of charming?'

'You shouldn't have broached the subject. Have whatever opinion you please, but keep it to yourself.'

'It is, however, very natural to say what one thinks.'

'Not in Society, my dear niece. Half the time one has

to say what one doesn't think and conceal what one does think.'

'What a frightful rule,' I said in horror. 'I shall never be able to put it into practice.'

'You will in time; but meantime conform to etiquette.'

'Etiquette again!' I retorted, getting angry.

In the evening, dreaming at my window, as I had acquired the habit of doing, my dreams were troubled by an obscure uneasiness which I did not succeed in defining satisfactorily. I thought about this day, which I had awaited with so much impatience. I could not pretend that things had turned out as I had wished. What had I hoped? I don't know, but I made myself a long speech to convince myself that M. de Conprat was in love with me, and I concluded my peroration with disturbed feelings.

Nevertheless, the next day my uneasiness had completely disappeared; in the afternoon, however, I received a long letter from the Curé, which was full of good advice and ended as follows:

'Little Reine, your letter came to comfort me and gladden me in my solitude; do not weary of writing to me, I beg you. I don't know what will become of me without you and I daren't go to "The Thicket", for fear of crying like a child. I reproach myself for my selfishness, for you are happy, but, as the Bible says, the flesh is weak, and my presbytery, my work and my prayers have still been able to comfort me.

'Adieu, my dear little child. My last word is to say to you, beware of imagination.'

And this phrase gave rise to an unpleasant feeling in my unsettled mind.

CHAPTER ELEVEN

I HAD been at Le Pavol for three weeks and my uncle pretended that I had got so pretty that it would be impossible for the Curé to recognize me if he met me. He compared me to a vigorous plant, which grows well on barren soil because it possesses character, and the beauty of which suddenly develops in incredible fashion when it is transplanted to a soil suitable to its nature.

When I looked at myself in the glass, I maintained that my brown eyes had a new lustre, that my mouth was fresher, and that my Southern complexion had acquired delicate rose tints, which gave me the liveliest satisfaction.

A few days after the lunch I have mentioned, however, I definitely discovered that in my extreme ingenuousness I had grossly deceived myself in thinking that M. de Conprat was in love with me. But I have never been a pessimist and I hastened to argue, in order to comfort myself. I reflected that all hearts are not necessarily alike, that some yield in a trice, but others are entitled to meditate, to study the situation before becoming passionate; that if M. de Conprat did not love me, he would do so one day or another, seeing that it was obvious that there was a real affinity between our tastes and our respective characters. So that, although the deception was great, my peace of mind, which lasted several days, was not seriously disturbed. And I became more cheerful in surroundings sympathetic to all my tastes; I warmed myself in the rays of my happiness, like a lizard in the rays of the sun.

My cousin was an accomplished musician. The Major,

who adored music, came to Le Pavol several times a week, and his son invariably accompanied him. Moreover, the doors were always open to him in virtue of his relations with Blanche when a child, and the relationship which united the two families. Furthermore, my uncle noticed this intimacy with pleasure, for, in agreement with the Major and despite his paradoxical views on the subject of marriage, he eagerly desired his daughter to marry M. de Conprat, considering, with sufficient reason, that the conditions constituted 'exceptional circumstances'.

I became aware of this project later, at the same time as other facts, which I should easily have discovered if I had had more experience.

As a general rule these gentlemen arrived for lunch. Paul, who possessed an appetite that has been described, lunched liberally and then ate a solid meal about three o'clock. After that, if we were alone, Blanche gave me a dancing lesson, whilst he played energetically a waltz of his own composition. Sometimes he became the professor: my cousin sat at the piano, the Major and my uncle looked on at us gaily and I whirled round in the arms of M. de Conprat in indescribable joy. They were wonderful days!

We made no plans without including him. His infectious liveliness, conciliatory spirit, genius for organisation and amusing inventions, which he possessed in the highest degree, made him a charming companion, who enlivened our life and increased my love. Clever, industrious, obliging, he was good at everything. When we broke a watch, a bracelet, no matter what article, Blanche and I said: 'If Paul comes to-day, he will mend it for us.'

He often painted and brought us his pictures. That is the only point on which I was unable to share his tastes. I had an inveterate antipathy to the arts, but above all to music, for cursed etiquette precludes one's stuffing up one's ears, whereas it is easy not to look at a picture, or to turn one's back on it. However, when M. de Conprat played dance tunes, I listened to him with pleasure and for a long time; but it was him I loved in his tunes and not the tunes *per se*. I note this feeling *en passant*, because one day I analysed it and this led to a terrible discovery.

'Why paint trees, Cousin?' I said. 'The ugliest tree is better than these little green patches which you put on your canvas.'

'Is that the way you interpret art?'

'Don't you think Juno is a thousand times more beautiful in real life than in her portrait?'

'Yes; I certainly think so.'

'What are those little blue flowers which you put in the trees?'

'Why, that's a corner of the sky, Cousin.'

I whirled round and exclaimed pathetically:

'O Heavens, O trees, O nature, what crimes are committed in your name!'

My uncle had numerous friends at V——; he was connected with most of the country families and kept open house. It was rare for us not to have a few guests at lunch or dinner. This arrangement enabled me to become acquainted with etiquette and learn, as the Curé told me, to balance my feelings. But I must say I did not show much balance and I hardly concealed impressions and thoughts which were both preposterous and impertinent.

My uncle and Juno, absolutely inflexible on the score of

propriety, gave me well-expressed objurgations, but that was idle talk! With a really distressing tenacity I did not lose the chance of committing a blunder, or saying something silly.

'You have been very impolite to Madame A——, Reine.'

'In what way, hypocritical Juno? I let her see that she displeased me, that is all.'

'That is precisely what is improper, my dear niece.'

'She is so ugly, Uncle. You see, I am not attracted by women; they mock, they are haughty and look at you from head to toe, as if you were a curious beast.'

'How can you reproach them with being scoffers, Reine? You spend your time in seizing upon the ridiculous in people and mimicking them.'

'Yes, but I am pretty; consequently I am allowed to do everything. M. C—— said so to me the other day.'

'I don't quite see the consequences. . . . Do you believe that men look at you from head to toe?'

'Yes; but it is to admire me, whereas women look for defects in my physique, and invent them, if necessary. You see, I have already noticed a host of things.'

'So we see, my dear niece; but try to observe that deportment is an appreciable virtue.'

When our male guests were young, they courted Blanche and me and I was very amused, but when they were elderly . . . ! Politics were discussed and they always gave me a sick headache.

These worthy people used to arrive extremely excited about some misdeeds of the Government; they spoke of them discreetly until the moment when a fiery Bonapartist exclaimed that he would shoot all Republicans, to strike them with terror. The *naïveté* of the remark made people laugh, but this imaginary massacre cleared the decks, sweeping away irritation and twaddle. We flung ourselves head first into politics and we dabbled in them until the meal was over. Everybody agreed that one should abominate a republic and republicans, but when each guest took out of his pocket a miniature government, which he had taken pains to bring with him, people lost no time in looking at one another furiously and becoming red as tomatoes.

The Legitimist was enveloped in the dignity of his traditions, his respects and regrets, and treated Imperialists as revolutionaries; the latter, in his innermost conscience, treated the Legitimist as an idiot; but as politeness did not allow him to express his opinion, he cried out like a man who has burnt himself, to make up for it. Then they fell again on the Republicans; they overwhelmed them with invective, deported them, shot them, executed them, beat them to a jelly. Bonapartists and Legitimists united in a common hatred to sweep these unfortunate bipeds from the face of the earth. People held forth passionately, gesticulated, saved the Fatherland, turned scarlet . . . which did not, however, prevent things, alas! from going their own sweet way.

My uncle, in the middle of these vagaries, interpolated an intellectual remark or common-sense observation from time to time and put the discussion on a higher plane than that of personal interests and individual sympathies. In no way a Legitimist, having moreover no preconceived opinion, he thought no less than this: that France, for nearly a century, has been walking with her head down and that, this posture being abnormal, she will finish by losing her equilibrium and by falling over a precipice, where she will be buried.

He laughed at the meanness and the stupidities of the

different parties, but he often had anguish of mind, which manifested itself in a droll remark. I have never seen him get angry; he preserved his calmness amidst various outbursts on the part of his guests, sure, moreover to have the last word, for he was just and saw far ahead. However, his antipathies were strong and he execrated republicans. Not that he was too passionate not to remain on a middle course; he might have accepted a republic, if he had deemed it possible, and deferred to the honesty of certain men, who struggle in good faith for Utopia.

I sometimes heard him call our legislators 'badminton players', comparing the laws which the two Chambers sent back to one another to shuttlecocks, which French-men regard with their noses in the air, floating about in sanctimonious manner, until the moment they fall on their respected cartilage and soundly crush it. From this I derived for my guidance various deductions, which I shall relate in due time and place.

M. de Pavol used to like conversation and even dis-cussions. If he spoke but little, he listened with interest. Beneath an artless exterior he hid general knowledge, well-defined, highbrow and delicate taste and sound common sense united to real loftiness of outlook. He was neither a saint nor a pious man. Like most men, he had his faults, I suppose, and made mistakes; but he believed in God, the soul, and virtue, and he did not consider incredulity, quibbling and a disparaging mind signs of virility and intelligence. He liked to listen to materialists and free-thinkers working out their systems, and he discussed them for a time whilst he watched the speaker from under the thick eyebrows which almost entirely hid his eyes. He then replied slowly, with the utmost tranquillity:

'Hang it, my dear sir, I admire you! You have almost attained the perfect humility preached in the Gospel. I am embarrassed not to be able to walk in your footsteps, but I have a devilish pride, which will always prevent my comparing myself to the caterpillar which crawls at my feet, or to a pig which wallows in my backyard.'

Always at loggerheads with the Municipal Council of his commune, he disliked the villagers and contended that nothing is more crafty and more villainous than a peasant. Furthermore, although he was esteemed and respected, he was not liked. Nevertheless, he gave generously to charity and performed acts of kindness whenever an opportunity arose, but he never allowed himself to be deceived by the petty trickery and sharp practices of the worthy farmers.

Lastly, though my uncle had not adopted any career, though he had been neither doctor, lawyer, engineer, soldier, diplomat, nor even a Minister, he fulfilled his mission in life, maintaining healthy traditions, respecting what is worthy of respect, not letting himself be carried away by the vagaries of the times, using his influence to lead certain minds into good and proper channels. In a word, my uncle was a man of spirit with a heart full of benevolence. I loved him very much and if he had never discussed politics, I should have considered him faultless. He adored his daughter and quickly bestowed great affection on me.

'What dreadful things governments are!' I said to M. de Conprat. 'They ought all to be suppressed; at least we should no longer hear politics discussed. Two things ought to be abolished: pianos and politics.'

'Upon my word, that just about fits in with my opinion,' he replied, laughing.

'Oh! you do not like the piano? But you listen with

pleasure to Blanche; at least you seem to, judging by appearances.'

'My cousin Blanche has real talent.'

This explanation made me feel the enervating sensation caused by mosquitoes buzzing round a sleeper: they annoy him without completely disturbing his sleep. Evidently the argument was not very plausible, for, in spite of Juno's talent, I, who disliked the piano, always wanted to cry out, or run away, when she played sonatas by Mozart or Beethoven. There are men who can boast of having bored humanity! I felt distressed when I thought of their wives.

In the middle of this agreeable life, of my hopes, my petty uneasiness, which vanished when countered by a kind word and the distractions of such a novel existence for a person like me, we reached the end of September. My uncle, with the gloomy face of a man who is being led to the scaffold, made preparations for taking us to the *conversaziones* announced by M. de Conprat.

CHAPTER TWELVE

I AGREE that my powers of observation were not exercised at my first ball. All that I recall of that evening is a feeling of delirious pleasure and the stupid things I said, because on the following day they earned me a severe reprimand.

From time to time Juno tapped me on the arm with her fan and whispered in my ear that I was ridiculous; but her attempts were useless, and I flew round in the arms of my dancing partners, reflecting that if waltzes are not allowed in Heaven, it is hardly worth while going there.

Now and then my partner thought it was clever to make efforts at talking to me.

'You have not lived in this part for long, mademoiselle?'

'No, monsieur; about six weeks.'

'Where did you live before coming to Le Pavol?'

'At "The Thicket"; in hideous country with a dreadful aunt who, thank God, is dead.'

'At any rate your name is very well-known, mademoiselle; there was a Chevalier de Lavalle besieged on Mont-Saint-Michel in 1423.'

'Really? What was he doing there, this Chevalier?'

'He was defending the place, which was attacked by the British.'

'Instead of dancing? What a great noodle.'

'That is how you appreciate your ancestors and heroism, mademoiselle?'

'My ancestors! I have never thought of them As regards heroism, I attach no value to it.'

'What has heroism done to you?'

'The Romans were brave, it appears, and I detest the Romans. But let us waltz, instead of chatting.'

And I tired out my partner.

My happiness reached its height when, in this brilliantly illuminated *salon*, under the very eyes of those women in their best clothes, in the midst of Society so far away from me such a short time previously, I found myself waltzing with M. de Conprat. He danced better than all the others, that is certain. Although he was tall and I was extremely short, his lovely fair moustache, twisted into points, occasionally caressed my cheek and I had a few temptations, which I shall not mention, for fear of scandalizing my neighbour.

Intoxicated with joy and the compliments which hummed round me, I uttered every imaginable and unimaginable nonsense, but I made a conquest of all the men and was the despair of all the young girls.

The *cotillon* roused me to a state of the liveliest enthusiasm and when my uncle, who had the air of a martyr in his corner, made a sign to us that it was time to depart, I shouted from one end of the *salon* to the other:

'You will only lead me from here at the bayonet point, Uncle.'

But I had to dispense with the bayonets and follow Juno, who, beautiful and dignified as always, hastened to obey her father without bothering about my recriminations.

When I had returned to my room, I undressed calmly enough; but in my nightdress and just before going to bed, I was seized with an irresistible urge. I took my bolster and began to waltz with it, singing at the top of my voice.

Juno, whose room was not far from mine, came into my room with a rather frightened air.

'What are you doing, Reine?'

'You can see that I am waltzing.'

'Goodness me! What a child you are.'

'My dear, if humanity had any brain, it would waltz day and night.'

'Come, Reine, it is cold; you will get ill. I beg you, go to bed.'

I flung my bolster into a corner and slipped between my sheets. Blanche sat at the foot of the bed and improvised a lecture. She endeavoured to prove to me that calmness, in all actions of life, is a great virtue, that each thing must be done at the proper time and in its proper place and that, after all, a bolster did not seem to her to be a very pleasant dancing partner and . . .

'As for that, I agree with you!' I said, interrupting her energetically. 'There are only dancers of flesh and bone who are serious and agreeable, especially when they have moustaches; fair moustaches, for instance! A little moustache which caresses your cheek whilst you waltz, that is really deli . . .'

Whereupon I fell asleep and only woke up at three o'clock in the afternoon.

When I had dressed, M. de Pavol asked me to go to his room. I immediately accepted this invitation, thinking that my uncle's brain had just evolved some lecture or other. From his solemn appearance I perceived that my conjectures were well-founded and, as I have always liked comfort both during the delivery of lectures and in other circumstances of life, I drew up an armchair, in which I stretched myself out comfortably; I crossed my hands on my knees and shut my eyes in an attitude of profound meditation.

After waiting two seconds and hearing nothing, I said:

'Well, Uncle, go ahead!'

'Do me the favour of sitting upright, Reine, and adopt a more respectful attitude.'

'But, Uncle,' I said, opening my eyes, astonished, 'I had no intention of showing you a lack of respect. I sat in a meditative position, in order to listen to you better.'

'You are making me lose my temper, my dear niece.'

'That is quite possible,' I replied quietly. 'My Curé often told me that I should make him die in harness.'

'Do you really think that I desire to go to the Devil because of a little ill-bred girl?'

'First of all, Uncle, I hope you will never go to the Devil, although you like him well enough; then I should be distressed to lose you, for I love you with all my heart.'

'Hum! That is fortunate. Will you now inform me why, after my lessons and advice, you behaved last night in such an unseemly way?'

'Give me details of your accusations, Uncle.'

'That would take a very long time, for everything you did was done very badly. Amongst other stupidities, when you observed M. de Conprat you addressed him by his Christian name; I was near you and I noticed that your partner considered that very strange.'

'I think he is capable of it; he looked like a goose!'

'I am not a goose, Reine, and I tell you that it was indecorous.'

'But he is our cousin and we see him almost every day. Blanche and I always call him Paul when we speak of him and even when we address him personally.'

'That constitutes intimacy, but not in Society, where everybody is not bound to recognize the parentage and relationship of other people.'

'Hence you must act in one way at home and in another in Society?'

'That is what I am trying to tell you.'

'That is hypocrisy, neither more nor less.'

'For heaven's sake, be a hypocrite. I do not ask for more. Finally, it seems that you told five or six young men that they were very nice.'

'It was quite true,' I exclaimed in an outburst of sympathy for my partners. So charming, so polite, so attentive! Then I got confused with my promises and I feared that I had broken them.

'In the meantime, you annoy me very much, Reine; for nearly seven weeks Blanche and I have tried to teach you that it is in good taste to control one's movements and the expression of one's feelings; nevertheless, you take every opportunity of saying or doing silly things. You have brains, you are a flirt, unfortunately for me your face is ten times too pretty, and . . .'

'All right,' I interrupted in a satisfied tone. 'That is how I like reprimands!'

'Reine, don't interrupt me, I am talking seriously.'

'Come, be reasonable, Uncle. On the first occasion that you set eyes on me, you said: "You are devilishly pretty." '

'Well?'

'Well, Uncle, you are well aware that you cannot always suppress a first impression.'

'That is possible, but you should try, and above all listen to me. Despite your extreme youth and your diminutive stature, you have the appearance of a woman. Try and have the dignity of one.'

'Dignity?' I said, astonished. 'To do what?'

'What do you mean, to do what?'

'I don't understand, Uncle. How can you preach dignity to me when the Government has so little?'

'I don't see the connection . . . What is this new fad?'

'But you maintain that the Government spends its time playing badminton; for a Government to do that, is frankly lacking in dignity. Why should simple individuals be more dignified than Ministers and Senators?'

My uncle began to laugh.

'It is not easy to scold you, Reine; you slip through my fingers like an eel. At any rate, I declare that if you do not wish to listen to me you will not mix in Society any more.'

'Oh! if you did a thing like that, you would deserve the tortures of the Inquisition!'

'As the Inquisition has been abolished, I shall not be put to the torture, but you will obey me, be sure of that. I don't want my niece to indulge in habits and behaviour which may be tolerable at her present age, but which later would . . .'

'Would what?'

M. de Pavol had a violent fit of coughing.

'Hum! Like a woman brought up in the woods, or something similar.'

'That comment wouldn't be so silly, as "The Thicket" and the woods are very similar.'

'Rest assured that I have been speaking seriously. Run away and reflect.'

For the nonce I saw that I must not joke during this formidable reprimand, so I shut myself up in my room, where I sulked for twenty-eight and a half minutes, during which period there arose in my heart the praiseworthy desire to make the acquaintance of the art of poise.

CHAPTER THIRTEEN

I SOON found out that proverbs sometimes do not usurp their reputation for wisdom, that in certain cases, where there's a will, there's a way, and that with a little goodwill I should be able to put my uncle's advice into practice. By that I do not mean that I committed no more stupidities, oh! no, that still occurred frequently enough, but I succeeded in sobering down and acquiring a relatively calm state of mind.

Besides, if my uncle had scolded me, it was rather, as he used to say himself, in anticipation of the future, for I was in a place where my acts and remarks were judged with the greatest indulgence. A place full of amenity, courtesy, polite traditions, in which, I had no doubt, I had a large number of relatives and connections.

Thanks to my name, my beauty and dowry, many sins against the proprieties were forgiven. I was *l'enfant gâté* of the dowagers, who related with delight anecdotes about my grandparents, great-grandparents and certain ancestors whose actions and gestures must have been very remarkable for those amiable marchionesses to discuss them with so much warmth. I discovered with satisfaction that ancestors count for something in life and cover with their dusty shield the licence and the whims of young descendants who emerge from the depths of the woods.

I was *l'enfant gâté* of prospective husbands who, in my eyes, saw my dowry shining brilliantly; *l'enfant gâté* of the dancers, whom my coquetry amused; and I confess on the quiet, very much on the quiet, that I experienced immense happiness in playing havoc with hearts and transforming heads into weathercocks.

O coquetry, what charm is enshrined in every letter of thy name!

This feeling must have been innate, for, after two or three *conversaziones*, I knew its details, its *nuances* and artifices.

I should like to be a preacher, just to preach coquetry to my congregation and refuse absolution to any penitents sufficiently devoid of judgment not to indulge in this delightful pastime. Perhaps I should not remain long in the bosom of the Church, but in my short career I think I should make a few proselytes. I pity men who, thinking they know everything, are unacquainted with the finest and most delicate pleasures. In my eyes, they lead the life of a gherkin, or of a melon at the most.

Whilst I moved about a good deal and revolutionized hearts, Blanche went her way, beautiful and proud, too sure of her good looks to take any trouble, too dignified to stoop to argument and the tricks which were a joy to me.

But when the first effervescence was over, I was very quickly reduced to reflecting that M. de Conprat was taking an interminable time to fall in love with me. He saw me from all aspects, in evening dress, in my Sunday clothes, as a flirt, serious, sometimes melancholy (rarely, I must admit), and, despite this diversity of aspect, which prevented the monotony of linking his fate with mine, not only did he fail to declare his feelings, but he seemed to treat me like a child. The Curé's remark: 'Rest assured he has taken you for a little girl of no consequence' began to trouble me a good deal.

In spite of my coquetry, pleasures and numerous

distractions, my love never for a moment decreased. My active life doubtless prevented my thinking all the time about it, and this explains my long period of blindness; but I never had any idea of finding a more charming man than Paul de Conprat.

However, at the court which beset my path, several suitors showed a real resemblance to the characters of Walter Scott which I so much admired. I many times asked myself how my great hero with the cheerful face and marvellous appetite could have moved me to such an astonishing degree at a time when my mind was under the influence of imaginary persons who resembled him so little. That is a psychological subject which I hand over to the meditations of philosophers, for I haven't the time to pay attention to it; I state the fact, I salute philosophy and I pass on.

On October 25th we had a final *soirée* at a *château* near Le Pavol. I wore a bright blue dress with two or three knots in my black hair and falling on the lobe of the ear. I was extraordinarily pretty and, on this particular evening, I was a tremendous success, such a success that during the following week five offers of marriage for me were made to my uncle. But I was uneasy, feverish, troubled and, contrary to habit, I did not enjoy the infatuation evoked by my beauty.

I waited for M. de Conprat impatiently, to look at him with eyes which were beginning to open. He usually arrived very late, with three or four young people from the fashionable country families. These gentlemen, being *blasé* from their earliest youth, and finding it extremely tiring, painful and distressing to waltz with pretty women, issued a few invitations in a bored, nonchalant and rather impertinent manner, except Paul de Conprat, who was too worthy, too natural a man not to dance with the satisfied air which circumstances required. I must say, however, that my high spirits dispersed the boredom of these unfortunate victims of experience, like brilliant sun dispels a light mist. I knew so well how to rouse them, exhilarate them, veer them round to all the winds of my caprices, that my uncle said: 'She is mad!'

Honi soit qui mal y pense.

I noticed with vexation that Paul often waltzed with Blanche, whereas he rarely invited me to do so and even then without formality or cordiality. I doubled my coquetry to attract his attention; but what did he care? His head and his heart were far removed from me and I took refuge in a distant corner, vigorously refusing to dance.

There was a time when I hid myself in the curtains which divided the large *salon* from a boudoir where several women were sitting, when I overheard the conversation of two respectable dowagers, whose conquest I had made.

'Reine is charming this evening; as usual, she is carrying all before her.'

'Blanche de Pavol is, however, more beautiful.'

'Yes, but she has less charm. She is a disdainful queen and Mademoiselle de Lavalle an adorable little princess from the fairy tales.'

'Princess is the right word; she is of good family and what would offend people in others is charming in her.'

'They say that the marriage of her cousin and M. de Conprat has been arranged.'

'So I have heard.'

For some seconds, the orchestra, the dowagers and dancers performed a nameless dance before me, and in order to avoid falling I clung to the curtain in which I had hidden.

When I had recovered from my dizziness, the brilliantly lighted *salon* seemed to me to be draped in thick crêpe; to the great surprise of Juno, I went to beg her to depart immediately, without waiting for the *cotillon*.

On my return to Le Pavol I said to myself: 'It isn't true, I am sure it isn't true!' Why trouble myself so much?

But I undressed, crying, with the idea that an immense misfortune was going to fall on me.

Nevertheless, as nothing is so versatile as a mind at the age of sixteen, the next day I resumed my hopes and treated the gossip of these ladies as of no importance. I determined to watch M. de Conprat carefully and I was in a state of mind which permitted the slightest indication to give substance to even past or transitory impressions.

In the afternoon of that unlucky day, we were all in the *salon*. The Major and my uncle were playing chess; Blanche was playing a Beethoven sonata and, stretched out in an armchair, I was looking, under my half-closed eye-lids, at the attitude and face of Paul de Conprat. Sitting near the piano, a little behind Juno, he was listening to her with a serious air, without ceasing to look at her. I found that this serious expression did not suit him and might justify one's calling him bored. My opinion was confirmed when I noticed that he endeavoured to stifle several little untimely yawns. It was then that I suddenly returned to my own satisfaction when he used to play dance music. I understood that I did not like the tunes, but the player, and that in his case, his feeling was exactly the same. He liked Beethoven all right, but he had fallen in love with Blanche and the antipathetic things in his nature pleased him in the person of the woman he loved.

Juno concluded her dreadful sonata and Paul said to her in a wave of enthusiasm, of which I knew the hidden motive:

'What a great master Beethoven was! You interpret his music to perfection, Cousin.'

'You yawned,' I exclaimed, leaping to my feet so abruptly that the chess-players made an angry complaint. 'I thought you had fallen asleep, Reine.'

'No, I was not asleep, and I tell you that Paul yawned whilst you were playing your confounded Beethoven.'

'Reine detests music so much,' said my uncle, 'that she attributes her personal ideas to other people.'

'Yes, my ideas have made me discover some fine things,' I replied in a trembling voice.

'What is the matter with you, Reine? You are in a bad humour because you didn't get enough sleep last night.'

'I am not in a bad humour, Juno. I detest hypocrisy and I repeat, maintain and shall maintain exclusively until death, that Paul yawned and yawned again.'

After this outburst I fled with the serenity of a whirl-wind, leaving the occupants of the *salon* plunged in astonishment.

I shut myself up in my room and paced up and down it, raging against my blindness and giving myself great blows on the head with my fist, just like Perrine when she was embarrassed. But these blows, beyond shaking my brain, have never provided a remedy for an un-fortunate love and, deeply discouraged, I let myself sink into an easy chair, where I remained a long time, catching cold and giving way to distress of mind.

As under all circumstances of this kind, I recalled remarks and details which, I reflected, should have enlightened me twenty times in each case. The predominant feeling within me, amidst many other very confused ones, was that of great anger, and my irritated pride, re-awakening, made me swear that no one should be aware of my sorrow. I was sincere and I firmly believed that it would be easy for me to hide my impressions at a time when I was in the habit of hurling them at people's heads.

I was going through one of those moments of irritation, during which the most placid individual experiences a violent desire to strangle somebody, or to break something. The nerves, which cannot be relieved by tears, need some relaxation or other, and I laid the blame on my terra-cotta men, whose grimaces and smiles suddenly appeared to me to be hateful and ridiculous. I at once flung them through the window, deriving bitter pleasure from hearing them break to pieces on the gravel of the path outside.

But my uncle, who was passing by, received one of the men on his revered head, happily covered by a hat and, considering the procedure a violation of all rules of etiquette, he replied with an apt exclamation:

'What devilish pastime are you indulging in?'

'I am throwing my little men out of the window, Uncle,' I replied, going to the window, from which I had been standing rather far back, in order to throw my missiles with more vigour.

'Is that any reason for breaking my head?'

'I beg your pardon, Uncle. I didn't see you.'

'Have you suddenly gone mad, my dear niece? Why do you break your knick-knacks in that way?'

'They annoy me, Uncle; they make me impatient; they get on my nerves! . . . Well, that's the end!'

I sent five of them out of the window at a time and, quickly shutting it, I let M. de Pavol rage against nieces, their whims and the disorderly state of his path.

In the evening he lectured me, but I listened to him with the greatest calmness; a wretched lecture, in the midst of my serious worries, producing on me the effect of a soap bubble bursting on my head.

After dinner I went to see my little terra-cotta men, which were lying in a pitiful state on the path. Broken to pieces! Reduced to dust . . . just like my illusions and my happiness, which I believed I had lost for ever.

CHAPTER FOURTEEN

PERHAPS you may be astonished at my lack of perspicacity, but who, without having my excuse of being only sixteen years old, has not given proof, at least once in his life, of an unbelievable blindness? I should like to know if there be a single man who does not feel a fool when he discovers a fact of which he has been unaware for a long time, although it was very obvious. Oh! it is easy to call oneself perspicacious! Easy to prove it when somebody dots the 'i's' for you. . .

It was real torture for me now to observe M. de Conprat, to perceive all the delicate attentions which he showed Blanche, knowing full well what the lively secret between them was. How I wept in secret, but never, I believe, did I experience a wave of jealous feeling against Juno. Goodness, no. I was a little creature who loved sincerely and deeply, but no shadow of angry passion was intermingled with my love. Only I was perpetually annoyed with M. de Conprat. He was the scapegoat, whom I blamed for my ill-humour, my sorrows and understandable bitterness. I did not cease to tease him and to say bitter-sweet things to him. Then I fled to my room, where I took giant strides up and down, making myself a speech.

'How intellectual it is to fall in love with a woman whose character resembles your own so little! He, so lively, as great a chatterbox as me for sure; and she, so serious, silent, a worshipper of etiquette, whereas he is sometimes bored with it, I can see perfectly. We used to suit one another so well. How is it he did not see it?

But Blanche is as good as she is beautiful; he has known her for a long time and after all, love does not depend on one's will.'

But these fine arguments failed to comfort me.

In the evening I sobbed in bed, sometimes even during the night, and, in spite of my laudable resolution to conceal my impressions, at the end of a fortnight the occupants of, and regular visitors to Le Pavol were astonished at my strange conduct. In the morning I was cheerful to the point of laughing for hours on end; in the evening I came to table with a gloomy air and I did not utter a word during the meal.

This silence, so contrary to my habits, caused great uneasiness to M. de Pavol.

'What is passing through your little head, Reine?'

'Nothing, Uncle.'

'Are you bored? Do you want to go on a trip?'

'No, no, no; I should be distressed to leave Le Pavol.'

'If you must adhere to your idea of marrying, my dear niece, you are free to do so. I am no tyrant. Do you regret the refusal you gave to the offers of marriage which have been coming in one after another for some time?'

'No, Uncle; I have renounced my idea and do not wish to marry.'

These unfortunate offers added to my worries. I could no longer hear marriage spoken about without desiring to weep. If M. de Pavol did not urge me to accept them, he made me perceive the advantages of each suitor and gently insisted that I should at least become acquainted with my cavaliers. He might easily have classified them as 'exceptional cases' and, amongst the numerous discoveries which I made each day, my uncle's inconsistency was not the one which astonished me the least. Inwardly I think that he was somewhat frightened at the 'cure of soul' which devolved upon him. But he left me completely free, and in order to refuse a few suitors, he was content with my reasons, which had neither rhyme nor reason.

'Why say such a lot about being in a hurry to marry, Reine?' asked Blanche.

'I shall not marry until I have found what I want.'

'Oh! And what do you want?'

'I don't know yet,' I replied with a catch in my throat.

Blanche took my face in her two hands and looked at me attentively.

'I should like to read your thoughts, little Reine. Do you love somebody? Is it Paul?'

'I swear it isn't,' I said, releasing myself from her grasp. 'I do not love anybody and when I do, you shall know it immediately.'

If death were not such a terrifying thing, I am sure that I might have been killed at that moment, before I confessed my love for a man who was in love with another woman, and that other woman my cousin. Fortunately there was no question of the stake or the guillotine, the sight of which would probably have destroyed my stoicism.

'Like you, I am going to wait.'

'I do not enjoy the same success as *mon petit loup* from "The Thicket",' she replied, smiling. 'Five offers at a time!'

'Don't talk any more about that, I beg you; it tires, bores and wearies me!'

Out of ill-luck a sixth cavalier, combining the rarest, the most extraordinary and the most complete virtues, suddenly joined the ranks of my adorers. Alas! I reaped what I had sown, for, since I entered Society, I had taken pains to relate to all-comers that I intended to get married as soon as possible.

My uncle sent for me and we had a long conference.

'Reine, Baron Le Maltour requests the honour of marrying you.'

'Much good may it do him, Uncle!'

'Does he appeal to you?'

'Not in the least.'

'Why not? Give me your reasons, good reasons; those you gave me the other day with regard to the gentlemen whom you refused there and then were worthless.'

'They were not presentable, your candidates, Uncle.'

'Come. M. de P—— was very suitable.'

'Oh! a man of thirty . . . Why not choose a patriarch?'

'And M. C——?'

'His name is so ugly, Uncle.'

'M. de N——, a boy of ability and very intelligent.'

'I counted his hairs; he has only fourteen at twenty-six!'

'Oh! and little D——?'

'I do not care for fair men. At any rate, he is a perfect nonentity. Once married, he would worship his face, his ties and my dowry, that's all.'

'I leave him to you, but I revert to Baron Le Maltour; what fault have you to find with him?'

'A man who has never danced anything with me but quadrilles, because I don't waltz in triple time,' I exclaimed indignantly.

'Serious cause for complaint, Reine. I repeat that I consider it ridiculous to marry so young; but in spite of your dowry and your beauty, it is possible that you will never find a man like him. He is a charming man. I have received the most favourable report about his morals and his character; an immense fortune, a title, a very old and honourable family . . .'

'Oh! yes, ancestors, as Blanche says,' I interrupted scornfully. 'I am frightened of them, Uncle.'

'Why is that?'

'They are people who only think of taking part in battle and getting their noses broken. What stupidity!'

'Oh! well, I know the Clerk of the Court at V—— thinks you are charming; he has no ancestors; would you like him to be informed that for that reason Mademoiselle de Lavalle is disposed to marry him?'

'Don't make fun of me, Uncle; you are well aware that I am patrician to my finger-tips,' I replied, taking the opportunity of admiring my hand and the tips of my slender fingers.

'That is what I think, if your appearance be not deceptive. Now, my dear niece, listen to me. You do not know Baron Le Maltour sufficiently to form an opinion of him and I definitely wish you to see him several times, before giving a final reply. I shall write to Madame Le Maltour that the decision rests with you and that I authorize her son to call at Le Pavol when he likes.'

'Very well, Uncle. It shall be as you wish.'

Five minutes later I was wandering in the woods, suffering from the most violent agitation.

'Oh! in that way this Maltour will be well received,' I said to myself, biting my handkerchief to stifle my sobs. 'In four days' time I shall wish him to get out of my life. And my uncle, who sees nothing, understands nothing. . . .'

I was wrong. In spite of my sudden pretentious hypocrisy, my uncle saw very clearly, but he acted wisely. He
could not prevent M. de Conprat from loving his daughter
and renounce the dream which the Major and he had
been indulging in for some time. Furthermore, quite
convinced that my feelings had not much depth and that
they were very childish, he thought the best remedy to
cure this caprice was to divert my ideas to a man who,
being in love with me, would know how to make himself
loved in virtue of the saying: love begets love.

The argument would have been perfect, if it had not
been fundamentally unsound.

Two days later Madame Le Maltour and her son
arrived at Le Pavol with a smile on their lips and looking
hopeful. The worthy woman said a hundred agreeable
things to me, to which I replied with the sinister, frown-
ing face of an *ostiarius* of the Jesuits.

The Baron was a fine boy . . . ; permit me to say that
by the use of that expression I do not wish to say that he
was a fool; not at all. He was intelligent and intellectual,
but he was only twenty-three. He was timid and very
amorous; the latter circumstance did not unsettle his
mind, but I should have been ungracious to have reproached him with it.

The next day he called upon us without his mother
and endeavoured to talk to me.

'Do you regret that there are no more *conversaziones*,
mademoiselle?'

'Yes,' I replied in as haughty a tone as Suzon's.

'Were you amused the other day at So-and-So's?'

'No.'

'Nevertheless, it was a brilliant affair. What a pretty
dress you wore. You like blue?'

'Obviously, as I wear it.'

M. Le Maltour coughed discreetly, to give himself courage.

'Do you like travel, mademoiselle?'

'No.'

'You astonish me! I should have thought you would have been an enterprising traveller.'

'How stupid! I am afraid of everything.'

The conversation lasted some time on these lines. Disconcerted by my laconic manner and the interest with which, with the most impertinent way in the world, I was following the movements of a fly which was crawling on the arm of my chair, the Baron got up somewhat red and cut short his visit.

My uncle accompanied him to the garden gate and, in a state of indignation, returned to find me.

'You cannot continue in this fashion, Reine. It is insolence both to me and to this poor boy, who is bashful and whom you disconcert completely. M. Le Maltour is not a man whom one can treat like a puppet, my dear niece. Nobody will compel you to marry him, but I want you to be polite and agreeable. Heaven knows you have a voluble tongue when you choose. Try and make it so to-morrow; M. Le Maltour will lunch here.'

'All right, Uncle. I shall talk, don't worry.'

'At least don't say anything silly.'

'I shall be inspired by science,' I replied majestically.

'What do you mean?'

'Don't get agitated. I shall do what you want me to do; I shall talk without ceasing.'

'It isn't a question of that. . . .'

But I let my uncle confide his thought to the *salon* furniture and I ran to the library to look for what I needed to carry out the idea which had just passed through my mind. I brought away with me the philosophy of Malebranche and a book on Tartary.

Malebranche nearly gave me delirium and I gave it up in favour of Tartary, which offered me more resources. I studied a few pages attentively until midnight, grumbling and cursing the inhabitants of Boukharia, who wrapped themselves up in such strange names. I succeeded, however, in retaining a few details regarding the country and several strange words, the meaning of which I did not know at all. I went to bed, rubbing my hands.

'We shall see,' I murmured, 'if M. Le Maltour will be successful under this trial. Ah! my worthy uncle, I have the upper hand, you may be sure, and in a few hours I shall have got rid of this intrusion.'

On the following day he turned up, looking happy and awkward, like a man walking on needles, but I welcomed him so graciously that he found a foothold on natural ground and M. de Pavol's uneasiness vanished.

The de Conprats and the Curé lunched with us. My heart felt oppressed looking at Paul talking gaily to Blanche, whereas I was condemned to endure the bashful attentions of M. Le Maltour, whose handsome face got on my nerves.

'I have changed my mind since yesterday,' I said to him suddenly. 'I like travelling very much.'

'I share your taste, mademoiselle. It is the most intelligent of pastimes.'

'Have you travelled much?'

'Yes, a little.'

'Do you know the Ruddar, the Schakird-Pische, the Usbecks, the Tadjics, the Mullahs, the Dehbaschi, the

Pendja-Baschi, and the Alamane?' I said in one breath, mixing up races, classes and titles.

'What is all that about?' he asked, bewildered.

'What? Have you never been to Tartary?'

'Why no, never.'

'Never been to Tartary?' I said scornfully. 'Do you at least know Nasr-Oullah-Bahadin-Khan-Melic-el-Mounemin-Bird-Blac-Bloc and what not?'

I added a few syllables of my own to the name Nasr-Oullah, to increase the effect, thinking that the shades of this worthy man would not emerge from the tomb to reproach me.

My uncle and his guests bit their lips to avoid laughing. M. Le Maltour's face assumed an expression of the most complete bewilderment, and Blanche exclaimed: 'Are you losing your head, Reine?'

'Not at all. I'm asking Monsieur if he shares my keen interest in Nasr-Oullah, a man who possessed all the vices, it appears. He used to spend his time slitting his neighbour's throat, throwing ambassadors into cells, where he let them rot; at any rate, he was endowed with energy and did not know the meaning of fear—a horrible defect, in my opinion. And his country—what a charming land. Every disease is prevalent and I shall send my husband there. Consumption, smallpox, vomiting which lasts for six months, ulcers, leprosy and a worm called "rischta", which eats you away; to get rid of it, you . . .'

'That is enough, Reine; let us have our lunch in peace.'

'What more do you want, Uncle? I feel attracted to Tartary. And you?' I said to M. Le Maltour.

'What you say isn't very encouraging, mademoiselle.'

'For people who have no blood in their veins!' I

replied disdainfully. 'When I am married, I shall go to Tartary.'

'Thank God you will not be free, my dear niece.'

'Yes, I shall, Uncle. I shall have my own way; my husband will never have his. Besides, I shall have him taken to Boukhara to be eaten by worms.'

'What is that? Eaten by . . .' murmured the Baron timidly.

'Yes, monsieur, you heard correctly. I said: eaten by worms, for, in my eyes, the most charming position in life is being a widow.'

The high and mighty Baron Le Maltour, although belonging to a race of valiant knights, did not stand the test. Understanding the hidden meaning of my Tartary whims, he went away and returned no more.

My uncle was angry, but I was unmoved. I danced a pirouette and said sententiously:

'Where there's a will, there's a way, Uncle!'

CHAPTER FIFTEEN

I KEPT my promise to the Curé and used to write to him regularly twice a week. This habit appeared to him so sweet, so comforting that when I suddenly interrupted the regularity of my correspondence, he became sad and uneasy.

Absorbed in my worries, I remained a fortnight without showing him any sign of life; then, yielding to his earnest entreaties, I sent him letters of this kind:

'Man is stupid, Monsieur le Curé. I have discovered that. What do you think of it? I kiss you, sending convention to the devil.'

Or the following:

'Oh! my poor Curé, I am afraid I have found out the source of the cold water we spoke about three months ago! Happiness does not exist, it is a trap, a myth, whatever you like, except reality.

'Adieu; if death did not make us so ugly, I should be content to die. To die; yes, Monsieur le Curé, that is what you have read.'

He wrote to me by return of post:

'My dear girl, what does the tone of your last letters signify? Three weeks ago you seemed so happy in the joy and glory of your success in Society! No, no, little Reine, happiness is not a myth, it will be your lot; but at present imagination has taken possession of you, it carries you away and prevents your seeing things in a just light. You haven't followed my advice, Reine; you have abused the bonfires, haven't you? Poor little child, come and see me, and we can have a chat together about your pre-occupations.'

I replied:

'Monsieur le Curé, imagination is stupid, life is rubbish, the world a piece of tinsel, bright enough at a distance, but, at most, good to put in a cherry-tree to scare the birds. I want to fling myself into a convent, my dear Curé! If I were sure that I should be allowed to waltz occasionally with charming gentlemen, such as those whom I know, I should certainly take refuge in one and bury my youth and my beauty there. But I believe that that type of distraction is not permitted by the regulations. Give me some information on this point, Monsieur le Curé, and rest assured that you are only an optimist, maintaining that happiness exists and is reserved for me. You are living the life of the rat in a cheese; not that you are an egotist, but you are ignorant of the disasters which can fall on the head of people living in the world.

'I have no illusions, my Curé. I am a little, old, stunted, cramped, shrivelled-up woman—morally, I mean, as I am prettier than ever—a little old woman who no longer believes in anything, has no hopes, and who reflects that the earth is stupid to continue to revolve, when its joys and dreams are swamped, pulverized and reduced to imperceptible atoms. . . . If one were to strip my moral personality of its worldly wrapping, which deceives the eye of an observer, I agree, I say that my moral personality is no longer anything but a skeleton, a dead tree, completely dead, devoid of sap, deprived of all its leaves and stretching out great stiff, thin arms towards the heavens. Provided the moral does not spoil the physical, Monsieur le Curé! I tremble at the thought of it! No longer to have the least illusion at the age of sixteen, isn't it awful?

'*Au revoir*, my old Curé.'

Two days later, after sending this letter, which ought to give the Curé a sad enough idea of the state of my soul, my uncle decided that we should spend an afternoon at Mont-Saint-Michel.

That day there was a breath of something evil in the air: I foresaw it. The evening before, the Major and M. de Pavol had had a secret and prolonged conversation; Paul seemed uneasy and nervous and my cousin was dreamy.

My uncle and Juno, who had an affection for Mont-Saint-Michel, showed me round it most agreeably; but, apart from the architectural art making the most limited appeal to me, I regarded things through the gloomy veil of my positively peevish humour.

'How tiring it is climbing all these steps,' I said, whining at every one.

'There are more than six hundred before one reaches the top, Cousin.'

'Then I want to stop here!'

'Come, my dear niece, you don't suffer from gout!'

And my uncle, climbing these steps, worn down by the tread of so many generations, told me the history of the Mount and the incident that befell Montgomery.

But what did Montgomery, these ramparts, this marvellous abbey, these immense rooms, the many souvenirs, asleep there for centuries, matter to me? I should take care not to revive them, as I had a hundred times more interesting things to notice on the face of this tall boy, who surrounded Blanche with care and kind attentions and yet gave no thought to me.

How stupid I was not to have seen his love sooner! He rhapsodized over the smallest stone, in order to be nice to her, and now and then I gave him a few black looks, which he did not even deign to notice.

'Ah! here we are in the *Salle des Chevaliers*. Come, Reine, what have you got to say?'

'If the knights were there, this room would be charming.'

'Don't you find it charming without?'

'Oh dear, no. I see large fireplaces, columns with little sculptured figures about them, but without the knights, whose heads might be turned . . . it's nothing.'

'I hadn't thought of that way of contemplating feudal architecture,' replied my uncle, laughing.

We crossed gloomy passages, which frightened me.

'We shall break our necks!' I groaned, clinging to the Major's arm, whilst Paul offered his to Blanche.

'We are sad, little Reine,' said the Major in a low voice.

'You talk like my Curé,' I replied with emotion.

'Come. Won't you confide in me?'

'I am not sad,' I replied in a peevish tone, 'and have no confidence in anybody. Suzon told me that men were nonentities and I share her opinion.'

'Oh! Oh!' said the Major, looking at me in such a kind way that I was afraid I should sob. 'So much misanthropy and such extreme youth!'

I did not answer, and as we arrived at a sort of long terrace I slipped away and ran to hide behind an enormous arcade. I rested my head on one of those centuries-old stones and began to cry.

'Ah!' I thought. 'How right my Curé was to tell me long ago, already a very long time ago, that one doesn't argue with life, but submits to it. All my logic is of no avail in the face of circumstances. It is so sad to be treated like a little girl of no consequence.'

And through my tears I looked at those much-vaunted beaches, which seemed desolate to me, this monument, whose height oppressed me and made me feel giddy; but, without accounting for it, I felt a sort of consolation in this mysterious affinity of a sad nature with my own reflections; in contemplating these immense walls, which shed their huge depressing shadows both on the earth and on the past.

On our homeward journey, when we were in the train, my uncle said:

'Well, Reine, taking things as a whole, what is your impression of Mont-Saint-Michel?'

'I think that one must die of fear there and get rheumatism.'

Along the road from V—— Station to Le Pavol, I reflected to what a limited extent things in this world are stable. Hardly three months ago I was following the same route under the influence of my happy dreams, in the intoxication of my joyous thoughts of the future I thought so beautiful . . . and now the road seemed to me to be strewn with the débris of my happiness.

It was rather late when we reached the *château*; however, my uncle took Blanche into his room, saying that he wanted to talk seriously to her that very evening.

I went to bed, crying my eyes out, with the conviction that the sword of Damocles was hanging over my head.

For some time Juno had been more human in her dealings with me. Every morning she came to sit on my bed and we chatted without ceasing. The next day she came into my room at seven o'clock with a calm, quiet step and that charming smile which used to transfigure her haughty face and which, perhaps, I alone knew well.

'Reine,' she said immediately, 'Paul has asked me to marry him.'

The thread snapped and the sword of Damocles fell on my chest. This king must have been devoid of common sense to attach such a heavy article to a single thread! Doesn't history speak of one hair? It is quite capable of it.

I doubtless expected this revelation, but as long as a fact is unconfirmed or unaccomplished, what human creature does not at heart retain a little hope? I went very pale; so pale that Blanche noticed it, although the room was half dark.

'What is the matter, Reine? Are you ill?'

'Cramp,' I murmured in a feeble voice.

'I shall fetch some ether,' she said, jumping up.

'No, no,' I continued, making a violent effort to retrieve my pride, which was in tatters. 'It has gone, Blanche, quite gone.'

'Do you often feel like this, Reine?'

'No . . . only sometimes. It is nothing, let's drop the subject.'

Blanche put her hand up to her forehead like a person who wants to drive out some tiresome thought. But I resumed our conversation in such a firm voice that she appeared to have lost her anxiety.

'Well, Juno, what do you expect to do?'

'Father tells me that this marriage fulfils all his desires, Reine.'

'Are you pleased?'

'Obviously the marriage pleases me; everything is suitable, but up to the present I have only liked Paul as a cousin.'

'What is wrong with him?'

'Nothing at all, except that he does not please me enough. He is a fine fellow, but I do not like that kind of man. Firstly, he is not handsome enough; then that Norman appetite lacks poetry, you must admit.'

'It is, however, quite logical to eat when you are hungry,' I answered, holding back the tears.

'What more do you want? I don't think that we suit each other.'

'So you will refuse, Juno?'

'I have asked for a month for reflection, little Reine. I am very puzzled, as I dread deceiving my father. Besides, from certain points of view this marriage embodies all that I can wish; and the man himself is absolutely estimable!'

'But as you don't love him, Blanche?'

'My father contends that I shall love him in due course; that, moreover, love in the real sense of the word is not necessary for marriage and to be happy in one's home.'

'How can you believe such a thing?' I said, jumping up indignantly. 'My uncle really has abominable views.'

But Blanche quietly replied that her father was full of common sense, that she had many times noticed that he was rarely wrong in his judgments and that she felt disposed to listen to him.

'Does Paul love you very much, Juno?' I murmured.

'Yes; he has for some time.'

'You were aware of it?'

'Without a doubt; a woman always knows these things. Hadn't you noticed it?'

'Yes . . . a little,' I replied, adding a smile full of melancholy to my stupidity.

Blanche left me, after explaining that Paul had delayed

asking for her hand in marriage because he was afraid of receiving a negative reply.

It was exactly what I was thinking feverishly, thinking that, influenced by her father, she would end up by giving her consent.

In her place, I should have said 'Yes' in a second and a fortnight later I should have been married!

Alas! my dreams were all over . . . and I became a prey to great discouragement.

CHAPTER SIXTEEN

IT was agreed that Paul should not come to Le Pavol for some time and, a thing which appeared to me unbelievable and unprecedented, Blanche, from the day she saw him no more, seemed disposed to marry him. We constantly talked about it, we even discussed the wedding dresses and I displayed an attitude of stoic resignation, worthy of the men of the classical age.

But this resignation was only apparent.

My discouragement increased, my eyes began to have black circles round them and I reflected that life being no longer endurable, separated from the man I loved, the simplest way was for me to quit this world.

Naturally the project was very painful, but I clung to it energetically; I meditated about it, caressed it with almost morbid joy. For instance, I swear on my honour that I never had the idea of asphyxiating myself, or taking poison, a method so dear to men of to-day. But, having read in some book or other that a young girl died of sorrow because of thwarted love, I decided that I should follow that example.

Having settled my course and my ill-humour confirming my gloomy thoughts, I decided that it was polite and proper to notify the Curé and that, for the rest, I could not die without shaking hands with him.

Having reached that determination, I entered my uncle's study one morning and begged him to let me go to 'The Thicket'.

'It would be better to ask the Curé to come here, Reine.'

'He wouldn't be able to, Uncle; he never has a half-penny.'

'It isn't very amusing to take you there.'

'Don't come, Uncle, I beg you; you would embarrass me considerably. I want to go alone with the old house-keeper, if you will allow me.'

'Do what you like. My carriage will take you as far as C——, where you will easily find a vehicle to take you to "The Thicket". When are you starting?'

'To-morrow morning early; I want to surprise the Curé and I shall sleep at the Presbytery.'

'All right, then. I shall send the carriage back for you in two days. Be at C—— the day after to-morrow about three o'clock.'

He looked at me attentively beneath his bushy eye-brows, rubbing his chin with a preoccupied air.

'Are you unwell, Reine?'

'No, Uncle.'

'My little niece,' he said, drawing me towards him, 'I have nearly reached the stage of wishing that my ambitions will not be fulfilled.'

I looked at him in great astonishment, for I always firmly believed that he had seen nothing.

I replied with much *sang-froid* that I didn't know what he meant, that I was very happy and that I wished all his plans to succeed. He kissed me affectionately and sent me away.

I therefore departed the next morning without wishing to accept the company of Blanche, who wanted to accompany me.

En route I reflected on my uncle's remarks.

'He knows everything,' I thought. 'How near-sighted I am with my expectations! But even if Blanche's marriage does not take place, what good would that do me, since Paul is in love? He cannot love somebody else now. I don't understand my uncle.'

I no longer thought, as I used to, that men could fall in love with several women. Judging by my own feelings, I reflected that a man cannot love twice in his life without providing the world with an extremely amazing phenomenon.

Having thus regulated the beating of my heart over the male sex, my ideas took another direction and I rejoiced at the thought of seeing my Curé once more. I resolved to fall on his neck, if only to prove my independence and the contempt I had for etiquette.

When I arrived at the Presbytery, I did not enter by the door, but through a hole in the hedge which I had known since time immemorial, and I crept stealthily towards the parlour window where the Curé was having lunch. This window was very low, but I was so diminutive that in order to look into the interior of the room, I had to climb on to a stump, placed against the wall instead of a bench.

I cautiously put my head into the middle of the ivy, which formed a leafy frame for the window, and I saw my Curé.

He was sitting at the table and was eating sadly; his cheeks had lost some of their colour and their roundness; his abundant white hair was not ruffled, as in former times, but flattened on his head with an appearance of indescribable desolation.

'Ah! my poor Curé!'

I leapt down from the stump, I flung myself into the Presbytery, losing my hat, and I entered the parlour like a bomb.

The Curé got up, frightened; his friendly face glowed with joy on seeing me, and it was not in order to contravene the traditions of etiquette but in an outburst of great tenderness and emotion that I flung myself into his arms and cried for a long time on his shoulder.

I am well aware that nothing is more out of place than to weep on a Curé's shoulder; that my uncle, Juno and all the dowagers on earth, in spite of my ancestors, would have covered their faces if confronted with such a scandalous sight; but I had been at the 'poise school' too short a time to have lost the spontaneity of my character. Besides, I hold the firm conviction that only stupid people, *poseurs* and heartless creatures claim never to sacrifice the laws of convention to a genuine, deep feeling.

'Life is a rag, my dear Curé, a miserable rag,' I said, sobbing.

'Have we really reached that stage, little girl? No, no, it is impossible.'

And the poor Curé, who laughed and cried simultaneously, looked at me tenderly, put his hand on my head and spoke to me as he would speak to a little wounded bird whose broken wing he wished to heal with caresses and kind remarks.

'Come, Reine, come, my dear child, calm yourself a little,' he said, pushing me away gently.

'You are right,' I replied, putting my handkerchief back into my pocket. 'For three months they have preached calmness and I have not profited from the lessons very much, as you see. Let us have our meal, Monsieur le Curé.'

I took off my gloves and my cloak and, with one of those sudden changes of mine, which had become common recently, I began to laugh, sitting merrily at table.

'We can chat when we have had something to eat, my dear Curé. I am dying of hunger.'

'And I have practically nothing to give you!'

'There are some haricot beans, I love them, and some home-made bread, which is delicious.'

'But you didn't come alone, did you, Reine?'

'That's true. The housekeeper is still sitting in the carriage behind the church. Send for her, Monsieur le Curé, and tell her to pick up my hat, which is blowing about the garden.'

The worthy Curé went to give his instructions and came back to sit opposite me. Whilst I was eating with great gusto, despite my tuberculosis and my pains, he no longer thought of having lunch and looked at me with an admiration which he vainly sought to hide.

'You think that I am prettier, Monsieur le Curé?'

'Well . . . a little, Reine.'

'Ah! if I went to confession, what huge sins I should have to tell you about! They are no longer the petty sins of the olden days which you know so well.'

And, without stopping eating, I related to him my vain pleasures, impressions, clothes and new ideas. He laughed and took snuff without ceasing with his former air of cheerfulness and looked at me indeed without any thoughts of scolding me.

'Am I not *en route* to hell, Monsieur le Curé?'

'I don't think so, my little child. One must be young in one's youth.'

'Young, my poor Curé! If you could only see into the depths of my mind! I wrote to you that I was only a skeleton, and it is true.'

149

'That is not apparent, at any rate.'

'We shall talk about it in a minute, Monsieur le Curé, and you will see.'

When I had eaten enough, the maid cleared away the things; we made a lovely fire and each of us sat in a corner near the fireplace.

'Come, Reine, let us now talk seriously. What have you got to tell me?'

I put my dainty foot in the glow of the hearth and calmly replied:

'I am *in extremis*.'

The Curé, somewhat startled, quickly shut his snuff-box, into which he was just going to put his fingers.

'You don't look as if you were, my dear child.'

'What? Don't you see my heavy eyes, my pale lips?'

'Why no, Reine. Your lips are pink and your face is flourishingly healthy. Of what are you dying?'

Before replying, I looked round me, thinking that I was going to utter a word which that modest room had never heard within its wretched walls, a word so strange that the old springless clock which stood in a corner and the holy images hanging on the walls were probably about to fall on my head in a fit of surprise and indignation.

'Well, Reine?'

'Well, Monsieur le Curé, I am dying of love!'

The clock, the images and the furniture remained impassive and the Curé himself only gave a little start.

'I was sure of it,' he said, passing his hand through his hair, which had resumed its dishevelled appearance of former days. 'I was sure of it! Your imagination has played pranks, Reine.'

'It isn't a question of imagination, but of the

heart, Monsieur le Curé, seeing that I am in love!'

'Oh! so young; such a child.'

'Is that any reason? I repeat that I am dying of love for M. de Conprat.'

'Ah! Then it is he!'

'Do you take me for a hare-brained creature, a giddy-pate?' I exclaimed.

'But, little Reine, instead of dying, you had better marry him.'

'That would be the logical course, my dear Curé; unfortunately I do not appeal to him.'

This statement appeared so extraordinary that for a few seconds he remained petrified.

'It is impossible,' he said, in tones of such conviction that I could not help laughing.

'Not only does he not love me, but he loves another girl; he has fallen in love with Blanche and has asked for her hand in marriage.'

I related what had happened recently at Le Pavol: my discoveries and blindness and Juno's hesitations. I crowned my account by weeping hot tears, for my distress was quite genuine.

The Curé, who could not decide up to the present to take my troubles and remarks seriously, looked terrified. He drew up his chair to mine, took my hand and tried to argue with me.

'Your cousin is hesitating; perhaps the marriage will not take place.'

'What does it matter, seeing that he loves her? One cannot fall in love twice.'

'That has happened, however, my little child.'

'I don't believe it; that would be dreadful. I am very unhappy, my poor Curé.'

'Have you told your uncle so?'

'No; but he guessed my thoughts. What is the good of it, by the way? He cannot compel Paul to love me and forget his daughter. I shouldn't wish him to know of my love; I should prefer to die.'

A long silence followed this display of my pride. We gazed at the fire like two sorcerers, who seek to read the secrets of the future in the flames and glowing coal.

But the flames and coal remained dumb and I wept in silence, when the Curé continued, half smiling:

'He does not, however, resemble either Francis I or Buckingham!'

'Ah! Monsieur le Curé,' I replied eagerly. 'If Francis I and Buckingham were there, they would need no requests to love me and I should be very satisfied with them!'

Hm! The Curé thought the reply was devoid of orthodoxy and full of unpleasant interpretations. As quickly as possible he abandoned the subject (which bristled with traps) which he had just broached and preached resignation.

'Think, Reine. You are so young! This trial will pass and you have a long life ahead of you.'

'I am not of a resigned character. Get that into your head. If I live, I shall never marry; but I shall not live. I am consumptive. Listen to that.'

And I tried to cough in a sepulchral manner.

'Don't joke about this subject, Reine. Thank God you are healthy.'

'Well,' I said, rising, 'I see that you don't want to believe me. Let us take advantage of this lovely weather and of the last moments I have to live to go to "The Thicket", Monsieur le Curé.'

We trotted towards my former home in the pleasant November sun, infinitely less soft and less warming than my Curé's kindness and the sight of his pleasant face, once again quite ruddy since my arrival. I looked with satisfaction at his hair, waving about in the wind, his brisk step, his whole figure, which I had watched for so many times through the window in the passage, corpulent and cheerful, whilst the rain lashed the window-panes and the wind roared and whistled through the dilapidated doors of the old house.

After a visit to Perrine and Suzon, I went from the top of the house to the ground floor. Indeed, time should not be gauged by the number of days which have elapsed, but by the liveliness and number of impressions. Only a very few weeks previously I had left the old ruin, and if people had told me that, since then, several years had passed over my head, I should have absolutely believed it.

I led the Curé into the garden. Poor virgin forest! It recalled sorrowful days; nevertheless, I derived pleasure from walking through it in every direction.

Then the recollection of a few delightful hours ran through my head; a memory still a delight to me, despite the bitterness of the disappointment which had followed a moment of happiness.

'Do you remember, Monsieur le Curé?' I said, showing him the cherry-tree Paul had climbed.

'Let us think of something else, little Reine.'

'Is it possible, my dear Curé? If you knew how much I love him! He has no faults, I assure you.'

Once launched on to this subject, no human or supernatural power could have stopped me, particularly as at Le Pavol I was obliged to conceal my ideas. I spoke at such length that the unfortunate Curé was quite dizzy.

We spent the evening chatting and disputing. The Curé enlisted all his oratorical talent to prove to me that resignation is a virtue full of wisdom and easy to acquire.

'My dear Curé,' I said gravely, 'you don't know what love is.'

'Believe me, Reine, with goodwill you will forget and easily overcome this trial. You are so young!'

So young! That was his theme. Doesn't one suffer at sixteen as at any other age you please? These elderly men are astonishing!

From my corner I said, shaking my head:

'You don't understand, you don't understand.'

The next day, whilst he was walking in the garden, I said to him:

'Monsieur le Curé, I have been pondering over an idea during the night.'

'Let's hear it, *ma petite*.'

'I want you to come and be the Curé of Le Pavol.'

'I cannot replace other people, Reine.'

'The priest of Le Pavol is as old as Herod, Monsieur le Curé; he is getting very old, and I am watching the signs of his impaired health with tender solicitude. Wouldn't you be content to replace him?'

'Obviously, yes; I should, however, be sad to leave my parish. I have been there for thirty-five years and I love it now.'

'Now? Hasn't it always appealed to you?'

'Why no, Reine; you know how gloomy it is. Perhaps you have never thought that I was young once. My dreams were not exactly the same as yours, *ma petite*, but I should have liked an active life; I should have liked to have seen and heard many things, as I was not un-intelligent and I should have wished to have intellectual resources, which I have always lacked. Besides, before you entered my life, I had no affection or kindness around me. You can, however, overcome boredom and every sorrow, Reine, when you want to. I had been very happy prior to your departure from "The Thicket"; I had forgotten the long days of my youth, which were so sad and so unpleasant.'

The worthy Curé looked in front of him somewhat dreamily, and I, who had never thought, seeing him cheerful and content, that he could have suffered at one time, felt moved at his genuine, sweet resignation, which was without the slightest bitterness.

'You are a saint, my dear Curé,' I said, taking his hand.

'Hush! Don't talk nonsense, my dear child. I have suffered from a suppressed existence, but don't you see it is the fate of all my colleagues, whose minds are young and active. I have talked to you about this, to make you understand that you can put up with anything, and regain happiness and cheerfulness when the trials are over and have been endured with courage.'

I understood very well, but the Curé was preaching in the desert. I was too young not to be arbitrary in my ideas and I naturally said to myself that in the face of sorrow, nothing can be compared with an unfortunate love affair.

'If the Curé of Le Pavol retires one day, I should be content to go there, Reine; only, this change does not depend on me.'

'Yes, I know, but my uncle knows the Bishop very well. He will arrange that.'

The Curé accompanied me back to C——. When he

saw me sitting in the elegant landau belonging to my uncle, he exclaimed:

'How glad I am to feel that you are in your seat, little Reine. This carriage suits you better than Jean's trap.'

'You will soon see me in a lovely *château*,' I replied. 'I shall perform my nine days' Devotions in order that the Curé of Le Pavol may go to Heaven. It is a very charitable idea, as he is old and suffering. You will have a beautiful church and a pulpit, Monsieur le Curé, a really large one!'

The horses went off and I leant out of the door to see my venerable Curé for a longer time. He was making me friendly signs, without thinking of putting on his hat, for a happy and joyous hope had entered into his heart.

CHAPTER SEVENTEEN

THIS visit to the Curé only did me good for the time being.

The salutary effect of his remarks rapidly vanished; I at once plunged into my gloomy thoughts, and my uncle, inwardly fuming against women, nieces, their evil brains and their whims, talked of taking Blanche and me to Paris to give me a little distraction, when, most fortunately, events hastened matters.

A few days later, M. de Pavol received a letter from a friend of his, who asked for permission to bring one of his cousins, a Monsieur de Kerveloch, a former attaché at an embassy, to the *château*.

My uncle replied cordially that he would be pleased to receive M. de Kerveloch and invited him to lunch, not doubting that he was anticipating the event which, engrossing his dreams, should tend to revive my joy and hope.

Two days later—I have good reason for always remembering that famous day—two days later, the weather was appalling.

As usual, we were all together in the drawing-room. Blanche, sitting in a dreamy mood near the fire, replied in monosyllables to M. de Conprat's remarks. This love-sick, obstinate fellow, unable to endure his exile, had reappeared at Le Pavol forty-eight hours previously. My uncle was reading his newspaper and I had retired to a recess next the window.

Sometimes I worked with nervous fervour, as I had a

passion for needlework; sometimes I looked at the over-cast sky, at the rain, which continued without ceasing; I listened to the roaring of the wind, that November wind which wails in such a doleful way, and I felt tired, sad, and without the least happy presentiment, although, at the same time, happiness raced towards me with the gallop of two fine horses.

Now and then I looked stealthily at Paul. He was looking at Blanche with an expression which made me want to strangle him.

'How absurd he looks,' I reflected, 'with his almost stupefied eyes wide open. Yes, but if I were in Blanche's place, if he contemplated me in the same way, I should find him charming, more attractive than ever. What stupidity, what human inconsistency.'

And I thrust in my needle with such anger that it broke clean in half.

At that moment we heard a carriage approaching the *château*. My uncle folded up his newspaper, Juno pricked up her ears, remarking, 'There is a visitor,' and a few seconds later my uncle's friend and the attaché were shown in.

I don't know why this title was inseparable, to my way of thinking, from old age and baldness. However, not only was M. de Kerveloch neither old nor bald but, apart from the portrait of Francis I, I had never set eyes on a man so well-built physically.

When he entered the room, I thought that some idea of matrimony was in his fine head. He was thirty years old; he was sufficiently tall to transform Paul, standing next to him, into a pigmy; his expression was intelligent and haughty, and of such a nature that nobody at the first or second glance would have bestowed upon him the halo of sanctity. Somewhat cold, but polite to the nth degree, he had lofty manners and a freedom which captivated Blanche there and then.

M. de Kerveloch looked at her with admiration and when, rising to depart, I saw him standing beside her, I declared with a secret joy that it was impossible to find a couple more suited to one another.

Everybody, I believe, inwardly made the same remark, for Paul left us with a gloomy face. Juno played the 'Dernière Pensée' by Weber, or something equally boring, ten times in succession, a sign in her case that she was very preoccupied, whilst my uncle looked at us one after another in a worried, sly way.

M. de Kerveloch came to lunch the next day at Le Pavol; three days later he asked for the hand of Blanche in marriage, and two weeks had elapsed after that event, when I wrote to the Curé:

'My dear Curé,—Man is a little mobile animal, changeable and capricious; a weathercock, which turns at every whim of imagination and circumstances. When I say man I mean mankind as a whole, for to-day I am the diminutive animal in question.

'I am no longer in a state of despair, I no longer wish to die. I think the sun has regained all its brilliance, that the future may well reserve some pleasures for me, that it is a good thing the world exists and that death is a stupid invention.

'Blanche is getting married, Monsieur le Curé, to M. le Comte de Kerveloch. Goodness me, how well they suit one another! And she was within an ace, an atom, or anything you like, of accepting M. de Conprat! A man whom she did not love, and whom she reproached for

having too hearty an appetite! Too hearty an appetite . . .
is this consideration ridiculous and isn't it rational to
eat when one has a hearty appetite? If you ask me how
events have suddenly developed in this way at Le Pavol,
I should have difficulty in answering. I am overwhelmed
and all that I can tell you is that one fine day, one brilliant
day—no, it was pouring, but it doesn't matter—one day,
I say, M. de Kerveloch arrived here, accompanied by a
friend of my uncle's. Seeing him come in, I guessed that
he would appeal to Blanche, for he has all the virtues
which she wanted her husband to possess. M. de
Kerveloch looked at her as a man who knows how
to appreciate beauty and, a few days later, he requested
the honour of marrying her, as my uncle and etiquette
would say.

'Juno has emerged from her usual nonchalance to
declare with warmth that no gentleman had ever pleased
her so much and that she definitely refused to marry M.
de Conprat.

'There you are, my dear Curé! It is obvious and clear,
and since then I have been dreaming of the stars as in the
past. I put a curb on my imagination, I let it trot until
it can run no longer, and I dance in my room when I
am alone. Ah! my dear Curé, I don't know why I love
you to-day ten times more than usual. Your delightful
face seems to be more cheerful than ever, your affection
more touching and kinder and your lovely white hair
more charming.

'This morning I looked at the leafless woods, which
seemed to be fresh and green, the overcast sky, which
seemed quite blue, and suddenly I became reconciled
with imagination. I shall repent all my life of having
treated it so shamefully the other day. It is a fairy, my

dear Curé, a fairy full of charm, power and poetry, which, touching the ugliest thing with its magic wand, adorns them with its own beauty.

'How the diminutive animal is changing! I can't get over it! On what do hope and joy depend? What is the good of getting distressed when things turn out so well without one's bothering oneself about them? But why am I so cheerful when nothing has been decided about my future and when I reflect that it is not possible to fall in love twice in the course of one's existence? What chaos, my dear Curé! There is nothing but mystery in this world and the mind is an unfathomable abyss. I believe that somewhere or other somebody has already expressed this thought, perhaps I read it to-day, but I am quite capable of saying the same thing.

'When my imagination has been allayed, however, my happy ideas are seized with an irresistible panic; they escape, fly away and disappear, without my being able in many cases to recapture them. For after all, Monsieur le Curé, he loves her! What a nasty word, applied in the way that I apply it just now!

'You told me that it was not a rare occurrence to fall in love twice in a lifetime. But are you sure of that point? Are you quite convinced? Love attracts love, people say; if he knew my secret, perhaps he would love me. Don't you, as a man of common sense, Monsieur le Curé, think that propriety is idiotic? A confession on my part would probably be sufficient to ensure the happiness of my whole life. Laws, invented by a mind devoid of judgment, prevent my following my inclination, my revealing my secret thoughts, and acquainting the man I love with my passion. To be quite truthful, I do not know, at the bottom of my heart, what would compel me likewise to preserve silence and . . . when I told you that the mind is an unfathomable abyss! My dear Curé, I perceive a succession of gloomy thoughts advancing towards me. How unstable man is!

'Circumstances doubtless alter cases. My uncle goes so far as to maintain that fools alone never change their opinions; but is the heart like the mind?

'Enlighten me, my venerable Curé.'

When a plan had been arranged, M. de Pavol did not like anything to upset its execution. Deviating from this principle, he decided that Blanche's marriage should take place on January 15th.

The disappointment had been a bad blow to him; but he had all the less idea of vexing his daughter, as he knew about my love. He was frank, loyal, reasonable and incapable of getting infatuated with a dream, when the happiness of his niece was at stake.

As for Paul, he bore his misfortune with great courage. Like the little one who loved him so tenderly without his suspecting it, he did not display the slightest desire to show temper. I guarantee that he never had any idea of poisoning his rival or readily cutting his throat in some corner of a solitary and poetic wood.

When he was aware of his blasted hopes, he came to see us with the Major. He shook hands with Blanche, saying in a frank and natural tone:

'I only desire your happiness, Cousin, and I hope that we shall remain friends.'

But this way of behaving like the hero in a comedy did not prevent him from being greatly distressed. His visits to Le Pavol became very infrequent; when I saw him, I found him changed mentally and physically.

Then I wept again in secret, getting indignant with

him. He might have been so logical as to love me! So rational as to see that our two characters greatly resembled one another and that I was madly in love with him!

Really, if men were invariably logical, the world would not be any the worse for it, or people's morals either.

CHAPTER EIGHTEEN

O N January 15th the weather was superb and very cold. The countryside, covered with white frost, had a fairy-like appearance. Juno, extremely pale, looked so lovely in her white dress that I was never tired of looking at her. I compared her to that cold and splendid nature which, dressed in dazzling white, seemed to be in keeping with her beauty.

After lunch she went up to her room to change her dress. She came downstairs again, deeply moved; we all kissed her pathetically, prior to her leaving for Italy.

'The great moment has arrived,' I mused.

My many emotions had tired me and I yearned to be alone. Leaving my uncle, therefore, to extricate himself from his guests as he pleased, I picked up a fur cloak and made my way to a spot in the park which I particularly liked.

This park was intersected by a narrow running stream; at a certain point in its course it grew broader and formed a waterfall, which stones, cleverly laid out, had made high and picturesque. A few steps from the waterfall a tree had fallen, its trunk beside the stream and its head on the other bank. It had been forgotten in this position and when, in the following spring, my uncle wished to have it taken away, he noticed that the sap was revealed by sturdy branches, which grew all along the trunk. He had another tree thrown alongside the first, had the branches tacked together, had creeper planted, which they trained on to the stumps and, with the aid of the weather, branches and creeper grew thick enough for my uncle to have an original, rustic bridge, which could be crossed only with the danger of entangling oneself in the branches and falling into the water.

This was the lonely spot, sufficiently far away from the *château*, which I had chosen as the *milieu* for my meditations. I stopped near the frost-covered bridge, in order to reflect on the future and to admire the huge icicles which hung from the waterfall, which the frost had arrested in its course.

I do not know how long I reflected thus, without bothering about the cold which stung my face, when I saw coming towards me the object of my tenderness, as Madame Cottin would say.

The individual appeared melancholy and in very bad humour. With a stick, which in a moment of thoughtlessness he had taken from my uncle, he was administering vigorous blows to the trees which were in his way, and the white dust which covered them scattered over him.

I half turned my back on him, but it is public knowledge that women have eyes in the back of their heads and I did not lose one of his movements.

Having approached me, he folded his arms, looked at the immobile waterfall, the bridge and the trees and did not speak. Busy with a little branch of fir spruce, which I had just broken, I held my breath, looking askance at him, without his perceiving it.

'Cousin . . .'

'Cousin?'

For a few seconds I awaited the end of the remark. But finding that he stopped there, I deigned to turn half round towards the speaker, to encourage him.

He frowned and exclaimed loudly:

'I want to blow out my brains!'

'All right,' I said drily. 'I shall attend your funeral.'

This reply surprised him so much that he let his arms fall and stared at me.

'You wouldn't prevent my committing suicide, Cousin?'

'No, certainly not,' I calmly replied. 'Why should I meddle in what does not concern me? I like freedom, and if you wish to quit this vale of tears . . . well, I shall not lift a finger to prevent your doing so. In this life let everybody act as he pleases.'

I then resumed studying my branch of fir-tree, whilst the object of my love, disconcerted by the easy-going way in which I contemplated his gloomy project, looked rather abashed.

'I thought you had a little affection for me, Cousin. The first time you saw me, you found me so agreeable.'

'Alas! Cousin, what does the opinion of a little country mouse matter, reduced to the society of a Curé, an ill-tempered aunt and a cantankerous cook?'

'That means that you granted me your favours simply because I wasn't in holy orders and because my face was not quite so faded as Madame de Lavalle's.'

'You are right, Cousin.'

He looked at me furiously, twisting his moustache with vexation and, picking up his hat with ill-humour, he hurled it on to the bridge. Oh! how well I understood the feelings passing through his mind. He was happy, happy to find an excuse to grumble and laying the blame on me for his disappointments, in the same way as I had vented my bitterness on my terra-cotta men and the wretched Baron Le Maltour.

'Your aunt was loathsome, mademoiselle,' he said suddenly.

'My lovely eyes made up for that, monsieur,' I replied in the same tone.

'And the well-stocked table. Everything was laid the wrong way!'

'Yes, and what a turkey! Why didn't you die of indigestion? I firmly believed you had, until I saw you here again . . . very much alive.'

'I know that it is impossible to have the last word with you, mademoiselle. I am not, however, an insufferable cousin. What have I done to you?'

'Why, nothing at all. I am giving you a proof of that by promising to accompany your body to its last resting-place.'

'My body!' he exclaimed with a painful shudder. 'I am not dead yet, mademoiselle. Please note that I shall not take my life and that I am leaving for Russia.'

'*Bon voyage*, Cousin.'

He had gone away and, thinking he had gone for a long time, I clasped my hands despondently and great tears trickled from my eyes, when I saw him retrace his steps, running.

'Come, Reine, let neither of us sulk. Why should we be angry? . . . Why, you're crying!'

'I was thinking of Juno,' I said, succeeding in talking in a natural voice.

'That is true, little Cousin. You are going to be very lonely. Give me your hand, will you?'

'With pleasure, Paul.'

Alas! he didn't kiss it, but he squeezed it sadly, for he was thinking of a more beautiful hand, which he dreamt of possessing.

167

And he took his final departure.

Despite the cold, to which I paid no attention, I sat down, crying, near the bridge and, bending over the stream, I saw my tears fall on the ice.

'To talk of blowing out his brains,' I murmured, 'he must love her tremendously! I know very well that he won't do so, but he is probably as much in love with her as I am with him, and I definitely feel that I could never forget him. Is it foolish to fall in love with a woman who suits him so little, whilst near him is a little . . .'

'What are you doing there, Reine?' said my uncle, who had approached me without my hearing his footsteps.

I quickly rose, ashamed at my inability to hide my emotion.

'Why, we are crying!'

'How stupid men are, Uncle!'

'Profoundly true, my dear niece. Is that why you are shedding tears?'

'Paul wanted to blow out his brains,' I said, crying.

'Do you consider him capable of resorting to that extremity?'

'No,' I replied, smiling despite my tears. 'Violence is certainly incompatible with his character, but his idea proves that . . .'

'Yes; I know. His idea proves that he loves my daughter; but, believe me, he will very quickly forget her, and when he returns here, we shall act in such a way that his heart no longer goes astray.'

'You are of the opinion then that a man can fall in love twice in his life without being a phenomenon?'

M. de Pavol stroked my cheek and looked at me with a sympathy aimed equally at my lack of experience and my sorrow.

'Poor little niece! Men who love only once in their life are as rare as Mount Aiguille-Verte.'

'Then man is a wicked animal,' I said with conviction.

But I was as delighted as I was angry and I only asked to take advantage of the meanness inherent in human nature.

'But Juno is so beautiful!'

'Look at this bridge, which you like so much, Reine. Before the branches and the plant which cover it have grown again, Paul will have forgotten; before the leaves have had time to turn yellow and fall again he will have returned to Le Pavol and . . .'

He smiled in an expressive way, then he went away without finishing his sentence and, quite thrilled, I watched him receding in the distance, thinking that uncles who foretell the future in that way with such assurance are indeed very strange creatures.

'That is all very well,' I mused, strolling back slowly to the house, 'but if his heart changes, he can fall in love with a woman on his cruise. Indeed, they say that Russian women are very beautiful. . . . He must be sent to the Eskimos!'

I began to run with all my might, and I arrived at the gate of the *château* at the moment when the Major was getting into his carriage.

I took him by the arm and led him aside.

'Is Paul leaving for Russia, Major?'

'Yes; his trip has been arranged.'

'I thought . . . if you wished . . . After all, it would be better . . .'

Decidedly it was very much more difficult to say this than I had supposed. My pride embarrassed me and counselled silence.

'Well, my dear child, talk quickly. I am freezing!'

'The die is cast!' I exclaimed at the top of my voice, stamping my foot.

My pride and I crossed the Rubicon, and I said, lowering my eyes:

'I beg you, my dear Major, to advise Paul to go and see the Eskimos.'

'Why the Eskimos?'

'Because the women of that country are hideous,' I stammered, 'and the Russians are very beautiful.'

The worthy Major raised my face, which was blushing with embarrassment, and replied simply:

'All right. I shall advise him to go and see the Eskimos.'

'How I like you!' I said with tears in my eyes, shaking hands with him. 'But tell him not to remain for long in the huts of those worthy people, for fear of catching a disease; it seems that the smell is atrocious.'

Seeing my uncle arrive, I fled, saying:

'Major, a man of honour has only his word; mind you keep yours.'

I went up to my room with the very unpleasant conviction that I had abundantly followed the Government's example and that I had just trampled underfoot all principles of dignity.

But if you didn't help yourself a little in life, how would you make your way in the world? This reflection silenced my remorse. I sat at my desk and wrote:

'Everything is over, Monsieur le Curé. They have been married and have departed, happy and overjoyed, and I would have given ten years of my life to be in Juno's place, with the individual you know so well. When will that be?

'Do you know what my uncle told me? He declares

that men who fall in love only once in their life are as rare as Mount Aiguille-Verte. I beg you, my dear Curé, to celebrate your Mass to-morrow with the intention: "that M. de Conprat be not the Mount Aiguille-Verte."

'*Au revoir*, Monsieur le Curé. I hope that you will soon come to the Presbytery at Le Pavol.'

CHAPTER NINETEEN

THE sole event at the end of the winter was in fact the induction of the Curé to Le Pavol parish, and I shall not stress the happiness which we experienced in our reunion without the fear of an early separation.

It was with delight that I saw him go up into the pulpit and preach cheerfully on the wickedness of mankind. Then he arrived at the *château*, as formerly at 'The Thicket', with his cassock tucked up, his hat under his arm and his hair blowing about in the breeze.

We resumed our chats, discussions and disputes. The time seemed long to me, and Juno's letters, which gave evidence of the most complete happiness, were not written to comfort me or make me patient. I also went constantly to see the Curé, to confide to him my worries, my uneasiness, hopes, and revolts against the period of waiting I was obliged to endure.

I knew that the man I was in love with had not, alas! appreciated the idea of going to see the Eskimos. He was calmly walking about in St. Petersburgh, and the beautiful Slavonic women made me very afraid.

'Are you sure that he will not fall in love with a Russian, Monsieur le Curé?'

'Let us hope not, little Reine.'

'Let us hope not! . . . Answer with more certainty! What are you thinking about? Come, he cannot fall in love with a foreigner; tell me that it is impossible and that he will love me one day.'

'I ardently wish it, my poor little child; but you would

do better by supposing the contrary and acting accordingly.'

'You make me die of impatience with your resignation.'

'What little wisdom you possess, Reine.'

'In my opinion, wisdom consists of wishing for happiness. Tell me that he will love me, I beseech you.'

'I ask for nothing better, my dear child,' replied the Curé, who, in spite of his dread of physical suffering, might have been capable of following the example of Mucius Scaevola and burning his right hand, if my happiness had depended on such a sacrifice.

Nevertheless, despite the joy of having my Curé with me, despite the kindness of my uncle and all those around me, I became extremely sad.

I loved to walk alone along the paths in the woods. I liked to remain for hours at a time near the waterfall, recalling our last meeting, thinking what I should do if I saw him appear, cheerful and charming, his eyes full of that expression which had made such an appeal to me at 'The Thicket' and which, since then, I had not seen again.

This love of solitude developed from day to day, and my melancholy increased in proportion. At last, I gradually lost my loquacity and if M. de Pavol had not, for a long time, taken my lovesickness seriously, that fact alone would have proved its depth in his eyes.

Six months passed in that way.

One day, on the anniversary of my arrival at Le Pavol, I was sitting in the Presbytery garden. Two hours previously a storm had refreshed the atmosphere and watered the Curé's flowers. He amused himself by looking for snails, whilst I, under the influence of attractive thoughts, leant my head on the wall near which my seat was placed and allowed myself to indulge in joyous hopes. The raindrops, which made the leaves droop beneath their weight, alone disturbed my reflections, and the smell of moist earth recalled the happiest hours of my life.

From time to time the Curé said:

'It is astonishing how many snails there are! Would you believe it, Reine? I have already found over five hundred.'

I raised my head heedlessly and looked at the worthy Curé smilingly, as he continued his search with eagerness. I then resumed my dreams and finally fell into a doze.

I was woken up again by the grinding of the gate which divided the hedge from the garden and the sound of a voice full of gaiety gave me the most violent shock I had ever felt.

'Good morning, my dear Curé. How are you? How pleased I am to see you! And Reine, where is she?'

Reine was still sitting in the same place, incapable of saying a word or making an exertion.

'Ah! There she is,' said Paul, approaching me with great strides. 'Dear little cousin, how delighted I am to see you again.'

He took my hand and kissed it. . . .

I assure you that what subsequently happened was beyond my control and you must not indulge in malicious suppositions on my account.

I declare that it was with all my might that I struggled with temptation; but when I felt his lips on my hand, when I understood that this action was not inspired by commonplace gallantry, but by a deeper feeling, when I saw him bend over me and look at me with an uneasy, affectionate, special, a hundred times more delightful expression than that which he had made me dream of . . . this was beyond my strength and fate, in which I believed from that moment, overcame me and flung me into his arms.

I had hardly time to feel the embrace which responded to my outburst. I took refuge, blushing and embarrassed, on the seat, hiding my face in my hands, without distinctly seeing the face of the Curé, whose expression, stupefied, frightened, and delighted all at once, remained later on in my remembrance.

'Dear Reine,' murmured Paul in my ear, 'if I had known your secret sooner, I should not have stayed away from you for so long.'

I did not answer, because I was crying.

He seized one of my hands and retained it in his, whilst overcome by a fit of bashfulness such as I had never had, I turned my head, trying to withdraw my hand.

'Let me have your pretty little hand; it belongs to me now. Turn your head towards me, Reine.'

I looked at those beautiful, frank eyes, which were smiling at me, and exclaimed:

'God be praised! My uncle was right; you are not Mount Aiguille-Verte.'

'Mount Aiguille-Verte?' he said, surprised.

'Yes, my uncle contended . . . but it doesn't matter. Who told you what you didn't know when you went away?'

'My father, M. de Pavol, and many things which I have recalled in the last two months.'

'It is true, then, that love attracts love?' I said innocently.

'Nothing more true, dear little *fiancée!*'

Oh! the sweet word; yes, we were engaged and we remained silent, whilst the Curé wept with joy and the sparrows on the roof of the Presbytery were chirping deafeningly and the snails, escaping from the prison in which the Curé had confined them, were moving about on all sides.

The sparrow is certainly not a seductive bird, its plumage is dull and ugly, its cry lacks melody and certain people accuse it of being a robber and immoral, which I refuse to believe; neither do I know that snails have ever been considered very poetical animals; it is none the less true that, ever since the moment I have mentioned, I have adored sparrows and snails.

I was filled with delight. I thought I was dreaming . . . I did not get tired of looking at him, listening to his voice, which I loved so much, and feeling his hand pressing mine. Nevertheless, whether I wanted to or not, the recollection of the girl he had loved haunted my mind and somewhat troubled my rejoicing, but I did not dare mention it to him.

'Does my uncle know that you are here, Paul?'

'Yes; I have come from Le Pavol, and I wanted intensely to come and be alone with you. Doesn't this damp garden remind you of something, Reine?'

I did not answer his question directly; I merely said:

'But as far as you are concerned, have you retained an unfavourable memory of "The Thicket"?'

'I, forsooth? I have never spent such an enjoyable evening.'

176

'Ah!' I continued, looking at him slyly. 'Was my aunt so horrible?'

'No, no, not so horrible. Rather *bourgeois*, perhaps, but you only appeared all the more charming.'

'And the table, which was so badly laid. Everything wrong.'

'I have never had such a good dinner. That shabby interior showed you off to advantage like a flower, which seems prettier and more delicate because the soil in which it grows is ugly and uncultivated.'

'You have become more poetical during your cruise,' I said laughing.

'No, not at all, little Reine.'

He put my arm in his and took me aside.

'No, not poetical, but in love with you, Cousin. Listen, I love you with the most heartfelt sincerity.'

I enjoyed the sweetness of this phrase and the look which accompanied it, musing that he was very happy and that men were fickle.

But this change seemed to me unprecedented and I could not prevent myself from murmuring:

'Are you quite certain that you no longer love her at all?'

'Should I be talking to you as I am doing if it were otherwise?' he replied in a serious tone. 'Haven't you faith in my loyalty?'

'Oh! yes,' I said, clasping my hands on his arm in a burst of affection.

It was quite true, for after his answer, Blanche's face no longer troubled me. I loved him without the slightest jealous or distrustful mental reservation, and he deserved this complete confidence.

'Look, my father and M. de Pavol are arriving.'

'Well, my dear niece, what do you think of my prediction?'

'You aren't very discreet, Uncle,' I said, blushing.

'It was the Major who revealed the secret, Reine; he had known it for some time.'

'Oh! no, only for eight months.'

'From the first day that I saw you, my dear little daughter-in-law.'

'Is it possible?'

'And Paul didn't go and see the Eskimos,' continued my uncle, laughing.

How happy one is living amongst worthy people! I felt this happiness keenly when I saw the satisfaction they derived from my joy and the delicacy and the kindness they showed when they teased me about that famous secret which, without suspecting it, I had thrown to the four winds.

Then commenced that delightful period of our betrothal, an exquisite period, like no other in life. Nothing replaces this time of ingenuous love, faith, complete illusions and childishness. Ah! how I pity those who have never loved in that way. How I pity those whose foolishness leads them far from the beaten track and legitimate affection. At any rate, whatever the eloquence of people who wish to convince me, I shall never, never believe that love can exist without esteem as its chief foundation.

We spent our most enjoyable time at the Presbytery, under the chaperonage of the Curé. We watched him walking in his garden, tying his plants to stakes, tearing up weeds and stopping his work to dart at us a look of *surveillance*, to show us that he was a serious adviser.

We watched him, laughing, for we knew the severity of our easy-going guardian.

I approached that worthy man, to rhapsodize with him over a flower, a small shrub, or some fruit and I said:

'Do you remember the time, my dear Curé, when you wanted to persuade me that love was not the most delightful thing in the world?'

'Ah! *ma petite*, I believe that "The Thicket" itself could not have convinced you.'

'Come, was I not right?'

'I am beginning to think so,' he replied with his charming smile.

My wedding day began radiantly. The sky had never seemed so lovely. Since then I have been told that the sky was very cloudy, but I don't believe a word of it.

A sympathetic crowd flocked into the church.

People whispered:

'What a pretty bride! How happy and peaceful she looks!'

Certainly I was astonishingly calm.

But why should I have been upset? My dearest dream had been accomplished, a happy future was opening before me and not the slightest anxiety ruffled me.

Indistinctly I saw a few dowagers smiling as I passed, and was filled with immense pity, as I reflected that they were too old to be married again.

The organ was being played so joyously that at that moment I became somewhat reconciled to my prejudices regarding music. The altar was covered with flowers and ablaze with candles, and every detail of the arrangements, carried out by Juno's artistic taste, charmed me.

My husband placed the wedding ring on my finger

with an unsteady hand, biting his handsome moustache to hide the quivering of his lips. He was more moved than I was, and his look told me what I should have loved to hear repeated for the rest of all time. . . .

And one might certainly have searched in vain all over the world and in all other planets in the universe for a face so radiant as that of my Curé.

Marcia Feuerstein